Secrets In Ink

Rebel Ink Book 3

Susan Harris

Originally published as Kindle Vella Episodes

Cover Design by: Gem Promotions
Typography by: Gem Promotions

PROLOGUE

Darren

DARREN WAS ABSOLUTELY WRECKED as he drove his banged-up Golf into the driveway behind his grans Micra a little after ten at night. He killed the engine and cracked his neck. His back ached, his neck ached, and he had a banging headache. All he wanted to do was to wash off the grime and fall face down on his bed and sleep for the next twenty-four hours.

Today at Rebel Ink had been absolutely mental.

Cathal was interviewing for new artists today, while he and Isaac carried on with their appointments. Shay had taken a day off from being apprentice to man the phones, and handle any customers that walked in. Their part-time front-of-house girl, Rylee, was off because her brother was sick.

While Cathal had advertised for experienced

artists, half the applicants had been looking to apprentice, and Cathal, who was not easily ruffled, was frustrated by the end of the day.

Darren and Isaac had been trying to handle what they could, but it had just been bloody insane. And Darren's client had been awkward, unable to stay still, and kept wanting to take a break, turning his four-hour piece into almost six.

Darren grabbed his bag, and noted that the lights downstairs were still on. His gran must still be up. It wasn't her bingo night, or her book club – which was just an excuse for her and her friends to drink and gossip, so she must have found something good on the telly to watch.

Darren locked his car and headed inside. Kicking off his trainers as he closed the front door, he heard the telly from the living room.

"Gran, it's only me." Darren called as he set down his bag and headed into the living room.

His gran was sat in her favourite chair, her head resting against the side. Her eyes were closed and Darren felt his lips curve. It wasn't the first time Darren had come home to find her asleep with the telly blaring, so he took the remote from the arm and turned it off.

Turning back to his gran, Darren walked over and put his hand on her shoulder gently, so not to startle her. "Gran, it's me. Time to go to bed."

It was then that Darren noticed that there was no

rise and fall in her chest, and his stomach twisted. His own heart began to race as he lifted a trembling hand and checked his gran's pulse.

Nothing.

Darren jerked back, his ass landing on the floor as he looked over at the woman who had raised him, the woman who had loved him when his own parents couldn't be arsed. Reaching out, he took her hand, and pulled out his phone to make a call. The sting of tears burned his eyes as he heard a voice ask what his emergency was, but he refused to let them fall.

"My gran," he choked out, keeping his hand in hers. "I came home, and she'd gone. She's fucking dead. I didn't know who else to call."

Darren numbly heard the man on the phone tell him that someone was on the way after he confirmed the address, but Darren just put the phone down, and scooted closer to his gran, rested his head against her leg like he used to do when he was a boy.

"I'm not ready, Gran. I'm not fucking ready to be on me own."

CHAPTER ONE

Darren

FOUR DAYS Later

The Irish certainly had a way when it came to funerals. For a people who were never in a rush to do much of anything, there was no dicking about when it came to funerals. Most were all done and dusted in three days, and then it was on to the wake, where stories were told and copious amounts of alcohol were drunk.

Darren had been numb to it all. He'd eaten only when Shay forced him to, and he'd pretend to sleep when Cathal had fussed over him. His friends had been amazing, helping Darren sort out all the details. But then again, his Gran had planned everything so that Darren wouldn't have to do much.

Darren remembered that his gran had told him she'd go down with her late husband, who had died before Darren was born. She'd left instructions with the hymns she liked, and what she wanted for the wake. She'd wanted no eulogy, thought they were stupid so instead Darren had asked Shay to read a poem, because he couldn't even speak for fear that he would scream.

The only thing Darren had to do was show up.

And try and track down his dad.

Darren hadn't heard from either of his parents in like ten years, and Darren was fine with that. They'd been happy to dump their newborn on his Gran, so he wouldn't interfere with their lifestyle. His Gran had sat him down when he was younger and been open and honest with him, telling him that his parents were selfish but that she loved him enough to make up for him not having a mam and dad around.

His Gran had been the one who noticed that he was good at art, who had gone out and spent a fortune on art supplies and never forced him to be anything but who he was. When he wanted to leave school to apprentice, his Gran had agreed only if she could come visit the place he wanted to work.

Then his Gran, with her blue rinse and cardigan, had seen what Barry was trying to do, had met Cathal, Isaac, and even little MJ, and she had turned to Darren on the spot and said he could jack in school.

She said it felt like a family and Darren would need a family when she was gone.

And now she was.

Darren's gut clenched as he stood by the window and looked outside. His Gran's friends were inside telling stories and it had just made Darren feel sadder than he already was. He hadn't cried yet, because he'd been afraid that if he started, then he would never stop.

That made him remember when he had come home from school one day, with a black eye and split knuckles, his eyes puffy with tears. Darren hadn't realised that not everyone was raised by their grandmother, that normal parents stayed home and didn't chose Dubai over their son.

Darren supposed that his gran was lucky that her son had been in Europe when she died and not in the Middle East. They had arrived in time for the funeral, his mam just saying his name as she slid into the seat behind him.

His dad said nothing.

Cathal had been standing next to him, dressed in an identical penguin suit, with Shay on the other side, holding his hand. Isaac was standing beside Cathal, and they had been standing beside him the last couple of days. His Gran had been right. His family were there for him when she was gone.

"Alright, cuz."

Darren glanced behind him to see his cousin grinning at him. Eve Andrews was his cousin on his mam's side, and one of his favourite people. Five foot three with a six-foot attitude, Eve had spent the last couple of years training in Liverpool, in a MMA gym. You would never think that gorgeous Eve would kick a man's ass but one day, she'd make it big, and Darren would be there to cheer her on.

"You decided to get a tattoo yet?" Darren said with a grin.

Eve snorted. "I'll let ya know when I do. You okay? I see your parents are as pleasant as ever."

Darren chuckled, roaming his eyes over Eve. "You look as comfortable in the black duds as I do. Or do you have your fight gear on underneath?"

Eve gave him a gentle shove. "I can wear normal clothes from time to time. I just wish it wasn't under these circumstances."

She reached out and gave his arm a squeeze, and Darren nudged her shoulder. "Your Da mentioned that you might be coming home soon? Be nice to see ya around a bit more."

Eve rolled her eyes, shifted her weight. "Ya, I'm negotiating with Rebel PR about repping me. And I heard Noah Donovan part owns an elite gym now so if I can get in there, I can keep an eye on ya."

Well, that was some bit of good news, Darren supposed.

"You should talk to Cathal. Declan Walsh is a part owner and he'll run it by Luna. Just don't tell her you had a thing for Cathal ages ago. Or do…damn, I'd pay money to see *that* fight!"

Eve laughed, then her Da called her away, and Darren knew she'd check in with him later. Even though she was training like a lunatic in Liverpool, she always found time to check in with him, with his Gran, and even though his Gran hadn't been related to her, she had insisted that Eve call her Gran too.

Hell, she'd forced all the lads and Shay to call her Gran too, which was hilarious since Cathal hadn't any experience with families, and there was his Gran ordering him about and hugging him. When he first started at the shop, his Gran had packed his lunch, and then made lunches for Cathal, for Isaac and even for Barry.

The thought made him smile, and Darren had nothing much to smile about the past couple of days. He wasn't really sure what to do tomorrow. Or the day after that. Cathal had ordered him to take time off, but the last thing Darren wanted was to be on his own, alone in the house, surrounded by Gran's things.

He'd left everything where they were on the night she'd died. Her mug that she drank her tea from, her blanket that she had crocheted herself and put over her legs when she got cold. The packets of mints that she hid in her crochet bag because she thought Darren didn't know they were there.

And Darren knew that if he opened the drawer of his bedside locker, that there would be a packet of

Haribo fizzy jellies that he liked hidden away for him to find. He couldn't face it, couldn't face that house and all the fucking memories that would come hurtling back.

"Never forget that I loves ya, Darren. Never forget that you can be whatever you want to be and never stop reaching for the stars. Because when I am gone, and you are sad, that's where I'll be, watching over you."

He'd always told his Gran to stop being so morbid, then kissed her on top of her head. He knew that she loved him. She had told him every day and he'd said it back. He knew that it must have been hard for her, a widow, and in her late forties to take on a newborn but his gran had done it.

Darren was the person he was today because of her.

Knowing that he'd avoided the wake for too long already, Darren took one more minute and then headed back inside the bar. He looked around, spotted Cathal and his friend inclined his head. Grabbing a beer from the bar, Darren braced himself for the small talk and the sincerities from all the people were bound to offer once they stopped him.

He noticed that no one had offer them to his Da though...which would have made his Gran laugh, and say, well, that's what he gets for being a selfish prick.

"Darren."

This was an interaction he'd been dreading since the moment his parents had walked into the church.

Darren had hoped they'd swan in and then fuck right off without any interaction. Darren supposed that considering how shite the week had started, this BS would only add to his misery.

Taking a deep breath, Darren turned round and faced the woman who had given birth to him.

CHAPTER TWO

Darren

HIS MA LOOKED how he remembered her, with just a tad less wrinkles in her no doubt recently botoxed forehead. Constance Fitzgerald wore a designer black blazer with a matching skirt, with high heeled shoes Darren knew probably cost more than his car was worth. Her make up was pristine, and she looked at him like he was no-one.

"Constance." Darren ground out, wondering how fast he could get away from her.

"Your father and I will be leaving later tonight."

"Right."

His Ma frowned, or at least Darren suspected she did, but he couldn't tell from her face. Constance looked over at his Da, then back at him, her expression one of irritation, and it reminded Darren of all the times when they'd come to visit his Gran and been completely bored by young Darren.

"He just wants to spend time with ya, Connie. You and Diarmuid."

"I don't know what to do with a child, Annie."

Darren watched from the stairs, peaking through the bars. His Ma had shouted at him when she had almost fallen over one of his Legos because of her stupid shoes.

"He is your son, Connie. He just wants to know ye. He's curious, is Darren."

His Ma let out a long sigh. "You were the one who told me that you wanted to keep him, Annie. I would have let that couple adopt him, but you were adamant."

His Gran snorted and shook her head. "As long as there is breath in my lungs, I was not gonna let some strangers raise my flesh and blood. If only you'd spend a little time with him, then you'd love him as much as I do."

"I don't have the capacity in me to love him, Annie. Neither does Diarmuid. We didn't want him."

Tears pricked his eyes as Darren felt his chest tighten. What was so wrong with him that his own Ma and Da didn't love him.

His gran tutted. "And what have you got to say for yourself, Diarmuid?"

"Connie is right. There's no room for a small child in our lives."

"That's fucking shameful, Diarmuid. I raised ya

better than that. Your father would be turning in his grave. That boy does not deserve to be ignored whenever you come to visit."

"Then perhaps we shouldn't come visit, Annie." His Ma said in a snooty voice.

"Ya, Connie, I think that would be for the best. Me and Darren will be perfectly fine without you both. Now, get out of my house."

Darren scrambled up the stairs, looking down as his Ma and Da just walked out the front door. He heard his Gran mutter good riddance, then she walked out of the front room before calling up the stairs.

"Darren, I know you're up there. Come down to me."

He did as his Gran asked, clamouring down the stairs to sit on the bottom step as his Gran came to sit down beside him. Darren picked at the strand of the carpet on the stairs, looking at the ground as he said. "It's okay, Gran. I won't be sad. I promise."

His gran took his hand. "You be sad if you want, Darren. You be angry or sad or anything else you want to be. I'm mad. I'm pissed as hell, but you and me are a team and we don't need anyone else. I'm sorry they aren't the parents you deserve, my boy."

Darren leaned his head against his Gran's shoulder. "It's okay, Gran. I don't need a Ma and a Da. Not everyone is as lucky to have a Gran like you."

"Are you even listening to me, Darren?"

The sound of his Ma's voice dragged him out of his

memories. Constance was looking at him with a disdain that Darren was used to by now.

"Is there something I can help you with, Constance? I just want to have a drink with me family and toast Gran. Safe flight or whatever."

His Da came over then, dressed in an impeccable suit but no emotion in his eyes. You'd never have guess that he had buried his mother this morning.

"Darren," he started, smoothing down the front of his suit. "We don't have much time in Ireland, so we just wanted to tell you that once we have spoken to our solicitor, we will put Annie's house on the market. You need to find a new place to live."

Darren's blood heated and his head started to throb. "Gran left me the house in her will. I have a copy of it. Her solicitor has a copy of it too."

"Yes, well, we will be contesting that." His Ma told him, no hint of emotion, like she was ordering take out and not talking about selling his home when his Gran was barely in the fucking ground.

"How fucking dare ye." Darren snarled loudly, loudly enough that people were looking at them. "Gran is barely six foot under and you are trying to go against her wishes. That was our home, mine and Gran's, not yours and if I have to bankrupt meself to fight ye on this, I fucking will!"

"Don't cause a scene, Darren. It's time that you acted like an adult. You can't sponge off the old woman anymore."

Darren felt a rage like he never had before ice his veins. He took a step toward his Da, his hands clenched. He wanted to make his Da bleed for the cold, callous way in he was talking about his own mother, and Darren felt like he needed to defend his Gran's honour.

Cathal stepped into his path, putting himself between Darren and his Da. His friend and boss put his hands on Darren's chest, his eyes understanding, but his touch firm.

"Let it go, Darren." Cathal said softly, in that calm, sometimes aggravating tone of his. "They aren't worth it and Gran would be the first to tell ya that if she was standing here. We'll fight them the right way"

Cathal was right, his Gran would hate him making a show of her like this. She wouldn't want this public argument. He'd fight them the right way and make his Gran proud.

Darren stepped back a fraction, but Cathal stayed where he was, angled toward them all. His Da went to say something, but his Ma stopped him with a hand on his arm. "We don't want to miss our flight, Diarmuid."

His parents turned and walked out of the pub without another word, and while it might not be the last time he heard from them if they wanted Gran's house, something inside Darren was absofuckunlutely certain that he'd never see the pair in person again outside of a courtroom.

Isaac came over and put a hand on his shoulder,

Shay nudging him on the other side. Eve strode over and ran her gaze over Cathal, his friend frowning at the unwanted attention. He had always been like that, unaware of himself until Luna.

"Jaysus, Cuz, I honestly thought you were gonna deck him." Eve grinned at him. "I'd pay money to see *that* fight!"

Darren barked out a laugh as Eve threw back his own words to him, then proceeded to tell him that she would be happy to show him how to throw a proper punch, when she came back to Ireland. She hugged him then, gave Cathal a wink, then headed off to where her own parents were standing.

Isaac gave his shoulder a squeeze. "How bout we make an Irish exit, get out of the corporate cosplay suits, pick up MJ, and go get some burgers? My treat."

Darren nodded just because he wanted to get out of there. He'd done what he could to make sure his Gran got the send off she deserved, and now it would be time for him to get used to his new reality, one where when he went home, his gran was no longer there.

Before Darren got in the back of Isaac's car, he took off his suit jacket, unbuttoned his shirt, and rolled up the sleeves. He started to feel himself again, but he couldn't seem to shake the tightness in his chest, and the numbness in his bones.

Shay got in beside him, and Darren looked away when he saw her and Cathal exchange a look. Isaac started the car, and then drove off, and it was only after a few minutes that he heard Cathal say. "Why don't you crash at mine tonight, Fitz? Shop's closed tomorrow anyways so we could hang out?"

Darren wasn't in the mood to be social, but he knew they wouldn't leave him alone until he agreed, so he mumbled a grand sure, and continued to stare out the window.

CHAPTER THREE

Nessa

900 SECONDS...900 seconds until the end of her shift.

Time had become Nessa's obsession. It consumed her every waking moment. And when she slept, if she slept at all, she woke up with a start wondering if today was the day that her ex would come to kill her. One miscount, one second when Nessa was exposed could lead her to being right back where she was the night Gavin had been arrested, the night he had almost killed her.

Glancing down at her watch, Nessa felt the panic well in her chest. She knew she should feel a little easier now that she was going to be moving into the upstairs apartment. But Nessa had been conditioned to always be hyperaware of the time, of her surroundings, and to never ever venture out during the day by herself.

It sounded crazy...but her life was crazy.

Nessa had been rebellious as a teen. Her parents were busy with their political aspirations, and Nessa had been forced to find ways to amuse herself. Nessa had partied hard, even at fifteen. Her parents didn't give her much of an allowance, so Nessa used to shoplift, mostly skimpy clothing and makeup. It was all about acting out hoping that her parents might spare her a thought.

Her parents barely spent an hour with her after the guards brought her home the third time she had gotten caught shoplifting. That same night, pissed off with her parents, Nessa went with one of her friends who invited her to an older boys party. The part of her that craved attention had been drawn to the tall, mysterious Gavin.

Gavin had spent the majority of the party watching Nessa. She'd felt the weight of his eyes on her as she danced with Maggie and Cara. Nessa was used to boys looking at her, wanting her, but Gavin was a man, and being wanted by him had made Nessa feel powerful.

It didn't take long for Nessa to realize that the moment Gavin decided on her, she would be the one to lose all of herself, lose all her power.

She had become a shell of herself.

Gavin had been everything Nessa had wanted in her life. He came from a rich family; he drove a flashy sports car. He was about to graduate college and then would go work for his dad's firm. He spoiled Nessa with gifts and trips, collected her from school, and made all her friends jealous.

It had started small... the controlling behaviour.

Gavin would get mad if she made plans with Maggie and Cara, then ghost her for a week before showing up at the school gates with flowers. He started to tell her that she didn't need to finish school because he'd look after her, and she'd never need to work a day in her life.

He put a tracker on her phone. Bought her less revealing clothes to wear. He begged her to move in with him, because he hated not walking up with her in his bed. Gavin told her that he loved her, that they were soul mates, and that he would die for her.

Nessa had been so swept away in it that when Maggie told her that Gavin was essentially grooming her, Nessa had gotten so mad, and they'd argued. Nessa had cut off all contact with Maggie and Cara, giving Gavin exactly what he wanted.

Nessa all to himself.

She'd been so blinded by Gavin that Nessa hadn't realized that Maggie had been right. The night they had met at the party, Nessa had been just shy of sixteen – Gavin had been almost twenty-one. Gavin had known how old she was that night when he had kissed her, then taken her hand and led her up the stairs. Nessa remembered his hungry eyes when he undressed her, when she popped the button of his jeans.

Nessa had wanted to have sex with Gavin. She wasn't a virgin, and sleeping with Gavin had felt exciting because he was older. The first red flag should have come when Gavin told her that she'd have to lie to adults and say they hadn't had sex yet.

The legal age of consent in Ireland was seventeen, and Nessa had been worried that Gavin would get in trouble, so she had agreed to keep Gavin happy.

Over time, Nessa had agreed to a lot of things to make Gavin happy.

She gave up her friends to make him happy.

She had moved in with him to make him happy.

She had decided not to go to college to make Gavin happy.

She had lost herself to make him happy.

When Nessa was firmly under his grasp, Gavin told her that his dad's shipping business was a front for the family business and that they were responsible for the biggest importation of drugs into Ireland. Nessa hated drugs and had been furious at Gavin for not telling her the truth.

That was the first time Gavin had hit her, splitting her lip, and giving her a dark bruise on her cheek. Gavin had kissed her and apologized, then taken her shopping once the swelling on her lip had gone down.

Then Gavin started to sample the drugs that he was dealing. He started drinking heavily. Nessa knew that when Gavin came in drunk she would either end up with another bruise or a broken bone, or naked under him until he passed out.

Six years Nessa had been with Gavin, and she didn't think there was any way out. One night she even considered stabbing him with a kitchen knife when he punched her for not cooking his steak the way he liked. It was all she could think as Gavin left her in a heap on the floor, cowering away from him.

So Nessa had looked up things online and decided to try spiking Gavin's beer with antihistamines. The sites online told her that mixing the two could result in making someone sleepy, so she tried, was amazed when Gavin had passed out on the couch before he could get angry about anything.

For six months, Nessa had a little taste of freedom. But that freedom always came with an axe waiting to swing at her head. Nessa started to make plans to leave him. She was in a chatroom online with other women and men in her position, and people who had gotten out. They told her to have a Go Bag. To have money stored away somewhere, in cash, so she couldn't be traced.

Nessa did all that, and was planning on leaving when Gavin had planned to go for a boy's weekend. She had hope for the first time in a long time. She knew what time Gavin was due to leave for his flight, what time his flight was due to depart, and how long she'd have to disappear before his flight landed and he called to make sure that Nessa was home, where he expected her to be.

Then Gavin had found the antihistamines.

It took less than ten minutes to beat her so badly that Nessa couldn't see through the blood in her eyes. Gavin had kicked and hit her, breaking her rib and when she tried to crawl away, Gavin broke her leg. Then he dragged her through the apartment toward the bathroom where he told Nessa that he was gonna drown her.

That she was his and would always be his.

When the guards had broken down the door and come to her aid, Gavin had just kept her head under the water until he was dragged away from her, and a young guard dragged her out of the water and told her she was safe.

Safe.

It was a novel word, wasn't it?

Because for the last two years since Gavin had almost killed her, Nessa had never felt safe. She'd gone to court like the guard had asked her. She'd testified. She'd felt sick to her stomach as she faced Gavin and he just smiled at her with a smugness that made her blood cold.

Gavin's family's influence meant that he was released on a curfew with a tag. Between ten at night and nine in the morning, Gavin was under curfew and couldn't leave the house. Nessa had clawed her way back and applied for the nighttime shift at Rebel Books.

Before she had agreed to move in upstairs, it took Nessa forty minutes to get home if she walked briskly enough. It took exactly two minutes to engage all the security features and another ten minutes before her heat stopped racing.

Glancing at her watch, Nessa sighed.

300 seconds until the end of her shift.

3600 seconds until Gavin was free and she was a prisoner.

Every day, over and over, until Gavin got the tag off and Nessa would have to decide if she had to run, or if she could stay.

87600 hours until Gavin could go outside at night. Ten more years.

CHAPTER FOUR

Darren

DARREN HADN'T BEEN HOME since the morning after his Gran's funeral. He couldn't face it. He felt like a right chicken shit for not facing up to it, but after two weeks, Darren had gotten into the routine of going to work, going for food, and then heading to Rebel Books to work on tattoo designs. He would then grab an hour or two of sleep in his car, before heading into Rebel Ink early to shower and change.

He could have stayed with Cathal or Shay, or hell even Isaac, but Darren hadn't wanted to bring them into his grief spiral. The first night after the funeral, Darren had gone to some random party, gotten langers drunk, then had fallen asleep in someone's bed. He'd been as sick as a dog the entire day, having ventured back home to shower, grab some stuff and then he was out the door.

Darren couldn't cope with being hungover and trying to filter his feelings about his Gran dying, his parents wanting to make him homeless, and the emptiness in his chest. His Gran had been everything to him, and now, now she was gone, and Darren didn't know what to do or what was the right way to feel.

He'd worked extra hours the past two weeks so that he had little time during the day to think. Cathal told him he could take some time, but Darren had been fucking terrified to have more time to think. Shay had sat in on a few of his tattoos, with her own sketchbook, taking notes and that, and while Darren knew she was learning how to be a full-time artist, part of it was her keeping an eye on him.

Their Rebel Ink family all had roles. Cathal was the dad of their family, making sure they were all sorted, and he worried about them like they were his own kids. Shay was the mammy, managing them and looking after them. Isaac was the older brother, the responsible one, who could sometimes lead you into trouble. That was before he had Melody and found his girlfriend Ciara.

And Darren...he was the youngest brother, the one always joking, always up to mischief. Shay had once called him a hyperactive puppy to his Gran and she had laughed, his Gran, saying that was an accurate description of him.

She had proudly hung all his work on her walls, even had the newspaper clipping of Darren standing outside Rebel Ink in nothing but his boxers when Cathal had been outed as a love interest of Heartache Melody's Luna Sullivan, his now girlfriend, and the media had swamped Rebel Ink.

Darren released a sigh, felt eyes on him and he glanced over at the woman glaring at him from across the room. He had arrived at Rebel Books early and taken over one of the tables in the gallery area, overlooking the main floor of the bookshop. He was hiding up here in case anyone he knew came in after he had told them all he was heading home.

His pencils and sketch pads were laid out on the desk, a bottle of Lucozade and a pack of Haribo jellies that MJ, Isaac's daughter had given him today. Then she had hugged him, and Darren had wanted to cry. He managed to keep it together as he thanked her, then let her practice her tattoo design on him with her sharpies.

Darren scrubbed a hand down his face as he tried to concentrate on the piece he was working on. He had all his designs for his tattoos for the week done so this was just a therapy piece that he probably wouldn't even show anyone. He'd been working on it for two weeks now, and it was darker than the stuff he normally did, but that was to be expected considering he was grieving.

The artwork was all black and grey, with various

shadings of light and dark. He had drawn a simple hourglass, but had it drawn so that there were fractures in the glass, with one crack large enough that some of the sand was falling out. A demon's clawed hand was grasping the hourglass, its mouth open as it devoured the sand.

It was supposed to symbolize that time was precious or something profound, but Darren just had drawn how he was feeling. He'd drawn the demon's eyes like his own, although he wasn't sure why he had drawn himself as the time-swallowing demon.

No, that wasn't quite right. Darren did know why.

His Gran had put aside her own life to raise him. She had never complained or resented him for it, but her life had been put on hold for him. Darren had devoured her time and now she was gone at a time when he could have been spoiling her like she deserved.

Darren ignored the glare from the student across the way as he slipped off his hoodie, and then pulled on his headphones to work on the tattoo. He spent time staring at it, wondering what was missing from it to finally be done with it. Drake's *Started from the Bottom* pounded through his headphones, his head nodding along with the music as he noticed movement out of the corner of his eye.

The woman who worked the night shift at Rebel Book, Nessa Kennedy, was serving a late-night customer at the till. The young woman said something to Nessa, and Nessa smiled, and Darren couldn't help but think it was the most beautiful smile he'd ever seen. Hell, Nessa was the most beautiful woman Darren had ever seen in his life.

Tonight, Nessa wore jeans that hugged her curves, well-worn Chuck Taylors, and a Rebel Books tee, with a green check shirt thrown over it. Her eyes were an intense shade of green that Darren wanted to paint on a canvas but didn't think he'd find the right colour to emphasise how striking they were. Her hair was a dark brown, with tiny streaks of caramel interwoven in the strands. Her skin was pale, but it was flawless. Nessa hardly ever wore make-up, but she didn't need it.

They'd been introduced a couple of weeks ago when Oli had roped them in to help haul some boxes up the stairs to Niamh's old apartment, where Nessa was apparently moving in. But Darren had noticed her long before that, on rare occasions that Nessa was at Rebel Books during the day, and Darren had been outside stretching his limbs after a long tattoo. But that day, Darren had noted how nervous she was around all the men, only relaxing when Shay had arrived.

He'd wanted to know who had put that fear in her eyes...

Darren had been attracted to her, then he heard her laugh at something Isaac had said, and he'd wanted to be the one to make her laugh, to take the fear out of her eyes. It was insane to be jealous of Isaac, because he was happy as a pig in shit with Ciara, and it wasn't like a girl like Nessa would ever look twice at him.

Flipping over the page of one of his sketchbooks, Darren stared down at the silhouette of a woman he'd been drawing for the last few weeks. He knew it was Nessa, knew that he was bordering on obsession, so he closed the book and lifted his gaze to where Nessa was sitting.

She was perched on the chair behind the counter, sipping a cup of something and reading a book that Darren couldn't quite make out. He wanted to know everything about her, what she drank, what was reading, what music she liked, what she looked and felt like naked.

Weeeelll okay, Holy inappropriate batman.

Nessa's head started to lift from her book, and Darren snapped his eyes firmly on the table in front of him so that he wouldn't make her feel uncomfortable if she caught him staring at her. Darren normally had no trouble talking to women, but there was something different about Nessa that made Darren nervous.

The music in his headphones changed to Kid Brunswick's *Baby I'm Not Okay,* and Darren went back to working on his drawing. He shaded in some more of the glass, then decided to add like an inky part at the end of the pages where the demon had crawled out of.

Then he stared at it for a time, his eyes burning as Darren yawned, and rolled his shoulders. He was just so fucking tired. The pages began to blur at the edges and Darren reached over and grabbed his hoodie, balling it up and placing it on the table as he pushed his sketch pad to the side. Resting his head on the hoodie, Darren rested his head down on it, and closed his eyes.

Darren felt exhausted right down to his bones. Maybe if he got a couple of hours of sleep, he'd be fine. Maybe after he slept, he would wake up and everything would feel normal again.

Maybe he would never feel normal again.

CHAPTER FIVE

Nessa

NESSA HAD BEEN PRETTY certain that the handsome tattoo artist from Rebel Ink had been staring at her, and had looked away the moment she had lifted her head to glance at him. Over the past two weeks, ever since Darren Fitzgerald had rocked up to Rebel Books every night, Nessa could feel his eyes on her.

It equal parts thrilled and terrified her.

For the longest time after Gavin, Nessa had never felt like she would ever want a man again, that she would never let herself be attracted to a man, but she was sure as hell attracted to Darren. The first time she had seen him, one night during the summer when she first started working at Rebel Ink, he had been laying on the bonnet of a car, naked except for a pair of basketball shorts, as Cathal, the owner of Rebel Ink, shouted at him to get back to work and stop sunbathing with no sunscreen.

Darren had just laughed, but he had rolled off the bonnet and grinned. Nessa had never seen someone look so carefree. It reminded Nessa of the girl she used to be before Gavin. But that girl was dead and the woman she was now wasn't about to let herself act on a silly attraction.

That was harder to do with him here every night.

Nessa found herself fascinated by his tattoos, by the ink on his skin. She wanted to learn all the secrets in his ink, find out the reasons for each tattoo, each placement, every... well...everything really.

The day that they had helped her move some of her stuff in upstairs, she hadn't been able to stop looking at him. He had a cheeky smile, dimples, bright blue eyes, and dark brown hair that was so rumpled, it made Nessa think that it would look like that when he got out of bed, when she had run her fingers through the strands.

And that was when she knew she was going insane.

Blinking away her foolish thoughts, Nessa glanced around Rebel Books, and she couldn't help but smile. Two years ago, after deciding that Gavin was not going to put a complete halt to her life, Nessa had applied for a job here, hoping to start a new life for herself, and she had found friends who didn't shy away from what happened to her, but embraced her.

Nessa had been terrified when she had gotten a call for an interview, knowing she had no college degree, or previous job history, but she loved books and wanted to start living her own life. Meeting both Niamh and Sorcha, who were warm and friendly, made Nessa feel like she could find her place with them.

Nessa fidgeted in her seat, her anxiety through the roof, but Niamh Kent seemed to notice, and she offered Nessa a friendly smile. "Don't worry, Nessa, you're doing great!"

Nessa wasn't so sure, but Niamh seemed so genuine, that she felt like she should believe her.

"Now, the role we have is mostly nights, but for every month you do a rotation of nights, we can swap it out so you do a couple weeks of days, if you like."

Sweat dripped own Nessa's spine, and she rubbed her palms on her pants. "I'd much prefer to just work nights, but I must leave at eight in the morning. I can't leave any later than that."

Niamh and Sorcha exchanged a look, and Nessa knew she'd lost the job there and then. She had no money, no proper home, and if she didn't get this job, she'd probably end up homeless. The guard who had helped her after her attack, he told her that it was vital that she get her footing because a lot abuse survivors ended up in another abusive relationship without a solid foundation.

He was the one who suggested the job to her when he had called to check up on her.

*"We would feel better if you had the option at least."
Blonde bombshell Sorcha said.*

Panic welled in Nessa's chest, and she couldn't breathe. Her head pounded as her entire body told her to flee. She heard Niamh tell her to breathe in through her nose, out her mouth, her voice calming and soothing, like she had dealt with panic attacks a thousand times.

When Nessa's lungs stopped burning, she lifted her eyes to the other women, and swallowed hard. She'd blown it, it was far too early for her to be trying to be normal again, and there was no way that they would offer her the job now.

"I'm sorry...I..." Nessa started, then gave herself a minute before she explained. "I've just escaped an abusive relationship. He almost beat me to death. He's on a curfew that means he can't be out a night, but by day, if he stays at away from me, he can still follow me. Public places he can explain away. I know he will kill me if he ever gets me alone. I'm sorry for wasting your time but I feel you needed to know why I need to work nights."

Nessa got to her feet, opening her mouth to thank them for the opportunity, but Niamh stunned her by saying. "Can you start next week?"

Nessa blinked. "I'm sorry, what?"

Sorcha grinned at her, asking her to sit back down and Nessa did. "What you just said, that took guts to admit to two strangers. The job is yours. But not as the shop assistant. We'd like you to take the night manager's role."

"I'm not qualified for that." Nessa blurted out, wringing her hands together. "I barely got my Leaving Cert, and Gavin wouldn't let me go to college. There must be other candidates with better qualifications?"

Sorcha grinned and flipped her blonde hair off her shoulders. "Have we interviewed people with more qualifications, sure...but none of them spoke with as much passion as you did when speaking of your fave book series. That's what we wanted, book lovers. And if you want to do something about the college degree thing, me and Niamh will help you with that."

Nessa looked at Niamh, who nodded, then said softly. "How long were you trapped?"

"Six years," Nessa admitted, feeling shame pinken her cheeks. "We met when I was fifteen and he was almost twenty-one. I got out three months ago when he almost killed me. I did some things to survive, but I want this job. I need it."

"Then welcome to the Rebel Books family, Nessa. And if you ever want me to track down the asshole who hurt you, just know that I'm a farm girl born and raised, and I knew how to castrate a bull. If that asshole has any balls, that is."

Nessa had been stunned by Sorcha's blunt words, as Niamh looked horrified.

"Sorcha!" Niamh exclaimed in a chastising tone as Sorcha just shrugged.

Nessa couldn't hold back her laughter, then the other two women were laughing along with her, and Nessa *knew she had found good people. She could start to rebuild here. She could be someone worth staying alive for.*

"Excuse me."

Nessa opened her eyes to see a woman standing on the other side of the counter. Since starting work in Rebel Books, Nessa had gotten less jumpy, less likely to scream when someone walked up behind her and tapped her on the shoulder. She was less afraid of shadows. It had taken time not to react, but she was slowly learning to temper her responses.

Plastering on a smile, Nessa angled her head. "What can I do for you?"

Nessa had seen the woman around a lot, saw her studying medical texts but she had always been quite curt and to be honest, looked down her nose at Nessa and the other staff. The woman was frowning, and Nessa hoped the woman wasn't going into anything that involved her dealing with patients, because from the sour look on her face, her bedside manner was utter shite.

"That man is snoring so loudly that I cannot concentrate. It's the same thing every night. Has he no home to go to?"

Have you? Nessa thought in her head, as she looked up to where Darren was indeed fast asleep. Nessa tried not to think of how adorable he looked with his head on his hoodie, but she dragged her eyes away and told the woman that she would try and wake him, and that Rebel Books was a space for everyone, and perhaps if she needed to concentrate, she could find a quieter place to do so.

Maybe Nessa needed to improve her own customer service skills.

Nessa went up to the balcony area, her heart racing as she walked over toward Darren, telling herself that Darren was not Gavin, and he wouldn't strike her for waking him. She tried to rouse him by saying his name, then a light nudge on his shoulder but he only grumbled.

The other woman had left so Nessa wondered if she should let him be, but her fingers traced the outline of the tattoo on his forearm in a moment of madness, and Darren's other hand snapped out grabbing her wrist and panic overwhelmed all her senses.

CHAPTER SIX

Darren

DARREN'S entire body seemed to come alive when he drowsily had felt fingers tracing his tattoo's. He was completely on autopilot as he grabbed the wrist of whoever was copping a feel while he was sleeping. Blinking open his eyes, Darren looked right into the terrified face of Nessa, and he yanked his hand back from her wrist.

Nessa seemed frozen to the spot as he pulled his headphones around his neck. "Shit, I'm fucking sorry. Did I hurt ya?"

Nessa took a step back, holding her wrist, her expression surprised like she hadn't expected him to care that he might have hurt her. And that made him hella angry at whoever had obviously hurt her before.

Green eyes darted to the door, then back at him, like Nessa was assessing if she could outrun him.

Shay told him that he could charm anyone with his smile, so Darren tried to do that with Nessa. Giving her a sheepish smile, he looked over to where the other woman had vanished, then back at Nessa, who was still frozen to the spot.

"Was I snoring? Karen doesn't like it when I fall asleep."

"Karen?" Nessa asked softly.

Darren chuckled, leaning back in his chair, and putting his hands on the table. He noted how Nessa glanced down at his hands, her eyes tracing the LOVE/HATE tattoos on his fingers. "Ya, that's not her name. I just called her that because she was always sighing at me. Like I was inconveniencing her. So Karen."

Nessa laughed then and Darren felt fucking invincible. She let go of her wrist, stopped laughing, then looked unsure as what she should do next. He wanted to hear her laugh again. He wanted to take that terrified look out of her eyes.

He knew he wasn't exactly the calmest person in a room, so Darren tried to reign in his tendency for chaos, and just be there for her.

"Hey, you want to sit down with me so I don't fall back asleep?"

Nessa pressed her lips together, and Darren made himself busy by putting his headphones away, and tossing his hoodie on the other chair beside him. he pushed his sketch pads a little away from him, giving Nessa the space to either sit down or walk away.

Darren really hoped she didn't just walk away.

Holding back his grin as Nessa pulled out a chair and sat down, actually angling closer to him, but so that she was facing the counter in case someone came in or needed help.

"You've been here a lot." Nessa said softly, like she was afraid that her statement would make him mad or something, when in fact, he was just happy she was talking to him at all.

Darren rubbed the back of his neck, snorted before he said. "It's really stupid. Saying it out loud will lose me serious cool points."

"Do you even have cool points?" Nessa retorted with a smile that quickly faded but Darren just barked out a laugh and grinned.

"Jaysus, you sound like MJ. She's always telling me how uncool I am."

"MJ is Isaac's daughter, right?"

Darren nodded his head, picked up a pencil out of habit and put it behind his ear. "Ya, she's amazing. Isaac's done a great job raising her. I love hanging out with her."

Nessa's gaze dropped to the Haribo, then back at him with a questioning smile. Darren pushed the open bag toward Nessa, urging her to take one. She slid her fingers inside, took out one and popped it into her mouth.

Darren was transfixed.

"Those were a gift from MJ to cheer me up. She says she's not used to me being sad."

Nessa frowned a little. "Why are you sad?"

Darren wasn't used to sharing his feelings, and he certainly wasn't used to spilling his emotions to a woman as gorgeous as Nessa. He ducked his head, rubbed the back of his neck, then shrugged. "Again, it's stupid. I don't want to go home. I've been living out of my car for a fortnight because I can't face going home."

Something strange flashed in Nessa's eyes, like she understood, and Darren wanted to know how she understood. But he needed to clarify exactly why he was hiding out in Rebel Books.

"My Gran raised me, " he told Nessa, his lips curving into a sad smile. "My parents didn't want me but Gran did. It was just the two of us for so long, and two weeks ago, I came home and she was gone. Died in her sleep they said. Peaceful. I should be glad it was peaceful but now I can't face the house."

Nessa was quiet for a little while, then she said "I'm sorry that you lost your Gran. I think you should look at it that you were lucky to have her. My parents were like yours, they didn't care about me, but I had no one to look out for me. So don't be sad that she's gone, be happy that you had her for as long as you did."

"Ya, I mean, I know I was lucky. Cathal never had anything growing up in care and then the streets. I was luckier than most people. I'll have to try to remember that when I'm being a misery guts."

Darren was looking at Nessa, but Nessa was looking at the drawing on his sketch pad.

"Is that for a tattoo?" she asked, lifting her gaze briefly landing on him before it went back to the grim artwork on the page.

"Not that one." Darren replied, reaching out to trace a finger along the outline of the hourglass. "That was just me messing about with designs I don't usually do."

"If this is something that you don't usually do, then I'm gonna need to see designs you do on a regular basis."

That made Darren grin as he pushed his sketch books toward Nessa, watching as she gently, almost tentatively. He noted the pictures that she stopped to pay more attention to, noted the ones she looked at and quickly moved on. Then it dawned on Darren that the sketchpad closest to him had drawings that Nessa might realize were of her.

With a swift movement, Darren slipped that under his backpack while Nessa was looking at his other sketches, because the last thing he wanted to do was look like an absolute weirdo if Nessa found out that he had been drawing her for the longest time.

Darren leaned his head against his fist and just

watched Nessa taking in his art. It was the one thing Darren had always known he was good at. His Gran had noticed too and sent him to art classes and she used to joke that he was destined to be a tattoo artist when he got in trouble in school for giving his friends sharpie tattoos.

Nessa gravitated back toward the piece he had been working on, unconsciously took another jelly as she popped it into her mouth, then she looked Darren right in the eyes. "Can I have this?"

"Eh, it's not done yet." Darren said, but Nessa shook her head.

"No, I think it's done." She worried at her lip. "I can pay you for it. But I want to hang this upstairs when I move in properly. I'll get it framed. Can I have it, please?"

Darren blinked, glancing at the A3 print, then back at Nessa. Whatever she had seen in the drawing had spoken to her, and Darren knew only too well how some pieces just took hold of you. He took the sketch book, and carefully pulled it out from the pad, and made to hand it over to Nessa.

"Have you signed it? I feel like it needs to be signed."

Darren chuckled, and grabbed a liner marker and signed it with his customary D Fitz, and then slid the drawing back over to Nessa. She looked at the signature, then at me with an intensity that it made him sit up straight.

"Thank you, D Fitz."

"You're welcome, Nessa K.." Darren said with a grin, and Nessa returned it.

"No, I mean it. I've always loved gothic art, like Anne Stokes. But I've never had the freedom to have something like this where I live. Thank you. If there is anything I can do to repay the favour, just let me know."

Darren glanced at his watch, saw that it was getting close to the end of Nessa's shift. "Come have breakfast with me."

Nessa jerked upright to a standing position so quickly, she nearly knocked over the chair. "No. I'm sorry but no."

She pivoted sharply and strode away as Darren got to his feet, ready to go after her and see if she was okay. One of the other staff came in, and Nessa disappeared into the office area, no doubt to avoid him.

With a sigh, Darren gathered up his stuff, pulled on his hoodie, and then made his way down the steps. In his hands, he had the sketch and the half-eaten bag of jellies. Stopping at the desk, Darren set down the art, and the jellies, asked the girl to make sure Nessa got them, and walked out the door, the little sliver of normality he had felt for the last hour slipping away.

CHAPTER SEVEN

Darren

FOR THE REST of the week, Darren stayed away from Rebel Books when he knew that Nessa was working, so as not to freak her out any more than she already was. He'd seen her going for lunch with Sorcha one day, and had noted the way she had glanced toward the tattoo shop before heading into the burger place down the road.

He had gone into the shop on the Sunday after getting a text from Cathal to stop by. It saved him driving around and wasting petrol trying to figure out what to do on the shop's closed day. Darren just figured that Cathal was bored and looking for things to do since Luna and the band were away in the UK doing some promo stuff.

He had barely parked the car when Cathal appeared,

along with Oli Scott. Darren thought it was insane that since Cathal was dating a rockstar, that he was now hanging out with rockstars and F1 drivers. Oli was ink obsessed, and his pregnant girlfriend Niamh who owned Rebel Books, called Cathal Oli's tattoo husband.

Darren grinned as he got out of the car, ignoring the look from Cathal as he spied the duffel bags in the back of his car. "Hey, what's the story?"

"We needed an extra pair of hands to help move the last of Nessa's stuff into the apartment," Oli told him, and Darren's stomach flipped. "I finally had all the security systems installed and they are good to go, so once we get the boxes up there, she can start making it her own."

A van drove up and stopped outside Rebel Books, and the man inside waved Oli over. Cathal fell into step beside him as they crossed the road over to the van. They lingered on the footpath, but Cathal was looking at him with that serious expression of his.

"What?" Darren asked, leaning against the wall.

"I stopped by your place last night with food. You weren't there. Mrs. Brown from next door said you haven't been home in a couple of weeks."

Darren snorted, rolling his eyes. "Old bat is probably in bed by the time I go home. You shoulda text me, I woulda met up with ya if I'd known you were looking for me."

Cathal ran a hand through his hair. "C'mon man,

it's me. I just wanna make sure that you're okay. It's been a rough couple of weeks."

"I'm grand, Hoggy." Darren lied his ass off. "You don't gotta worry about me."

Cathal chuckled, this time it was him that rolled his eyes. "You know me, Fitz, I'm gonna worry anyway. How bout you stay over at mine tonight, and we watch a movie and get food?"

Darren was about to answer when the side door opened, and Nessa and Cliona popped their heads out. Nessa roamed her eyes over the people outside. When they landed on Darren, she blinked, as if surprised that he would be here.

"Right, lads, shift your asses and move some boxes!" Cliona said cheerfully, and Oli laughed, telling Cliona that she was spending far too much time with Dani. Danika Keane was Oli's best friend, Cliona's girlfriend, and a rockstar in her own right.

"Dani is definitely a bad influence on you, Cliona." Oli teased going around the back of the van to start grabbing some boxes.

Nessa was still looking at Darren as he pushed off the wall, letting Oli pile boxes into his arms before he nodded at Nessa, gave her a small smile, grabbed a few boxes himself, and then went up the stairs. Darren followed Oli up the stairs, and then into the apartment. He set the boxes down on the ground in the living area, and rinsed and repeated until the van was empty and they had brought the last of the boxes up the stairs.

Darren set his box down and stretched. "Someone needs to ask Nessa if any of these boxes need to go onto another room or something. Some of that shit is heavy."

Cathal didn't respond as Oli came in with the girls, but Cathal was looking at the wall. Darren stepped around him and stopped dead. On the wall, in a black timber frame was his drawing. His heart galloped in his chest as Cathal looked at him, then back at the artwork.

"Why has Nessa got a framed piece of your artwork hanging on the wall, Fitz?"

The entire room was quiet as Darren muttered that Cathal needed to mind his own business. Oli looked from Darren to Nessa, his lips twitching like he was trying hard not to smile. Darren looked over his shoulder at Nessa, her eyes wide like she hadn't realized anyone would know who had drawn the picture.

Darren chuckled softly, hoping to divert some of the attention. "Jaysus, it's not a big deal. I was at Rebel Books, and Nessa saw the design and asked to have it. Simple as."

Nessa looked relieved as Darren glanced at her. "It looks good in the black frame. I'm gonna have to do some more to fit in with your aesthetic. Lemmie know if you have anything in mind. I take payments in Haribo and beer."

Nessa laughed but Cathal was still looking at him like he was trying to figure out the best placement for a tattoo. Oli told Nessa he wanted to go through some of the security stuff with her, so they disappeared into the bedroom, leaving Darren alone with Cathal and Cliona.

"Darren..." Cathal started, but Cliona was smiling as she leaned against the breakfast counter.

"Don't "Darren" me, Hoggy in that dad tone of yours."

"I'm not," Cathal mumbled, looking very miffed.

"Ya, you kinda are, Cathal." Cliona butted in, coming to Darren's defense. Darren grinned at her, then looked toward where Nessa and Oli had gone.

"Right, so can we just not make a big deal about the picture and make it bigger than it is? Last thing Nessa needs is you lot jumping to conclusions. Stop being nosy and let it go."

From the glint in Cliona's eyes and the look of suspicion on Cathal's face said that no one believed him in the slightest and his little statement had only made things worse. Darren was about to tell them all to fuck right off, when Nessa and Oli came out of the bedroom, and Oli showed Nessa the security panel on the wall by the door.

He and Cathal stood around like spare parts for a few minutes, then Oli told them that he owed both himself and Darren a pint, and that there was a high stool waiting for them at Sullivan's bar. They made to head out, and Darren wanted to say goodbye to Nessa without getting any more funny looks.

"Darren, can I have a quick word?" He heard Nessa say, almost flushed at the pointed looks from the others. Cathal said nothing as he left the apartment, then Oli who was grinning, and Cliona excused herself and headed into the bedroom, closing the door behind her.

Darren lingered in the doorway, leaning against the frame as he allowed himself one brief moment to roam his eyes over Nessa. She was wearing a plain black tee and leggings with those Chuck Taylors of hers. Her hair was pulled back off her face, the vivid green of her eyes staring directly at him.

She ducked her head, almost shyly. "I wanted to say sorry. About the other night. You were being nice and I overreacted."

"It's grand, really," Darren told her, looking over at the picture. "I meant what I said though. If you want that is. I can do some more stuff for the walls if you want. Once you've got everything sorted."

Nessa gave him a coy smile. "Yes, I'd like that. But only if you have time."

She could ask him to paint the ceiling a boring fucking beige and Darren suspected he would be down the DIY to get the paint before she stopped speaking.

"I've got time. Just let me know what you'd like and I'll start working on it. Maybe, if it's okay with you, I can come to Rebel Books some night and you can tell me what you have in mind."

"You stayed away because I freaked out," Nessa said, her words not a question more a statement.

"I stayed away because I didn't want to be the reason why you were freaked out."

Nessa shifted her weight as Cathal called up the stairs to tell him to hurry up. Darren flashed Nessa a grin, then shrugged his shoulders. "I better go before Cathal has an aneurysm. I swear he was born an old man who worries. If ya need any more help with things, gimmie a shout."

"I might just do that. I'm working Monday to Friday next week if you find yourself looking for somewhere to be."

Darren accepted the gift Nessa was giving him, a chance at friendship, and Darren would take it...because he wanted to know Nessa Kennedy's secrets. He wanted to know all of her and uncover the woman behind the fear.

CHAPTER EIGHT

Nessa

IT HAD TAKEN Nessa a couple of nights to get used to sleeping in the apartment. Everything felt so different here. Quieter, even during the daytime when she was trying to sleep. She had gotten used to the creak of the stairs leading up to her old apartment, the sound of the door when opened, letting out a shrill squeak. She knew that her neighbour watched reruns of Judge Judy in the afternoons.

And Nessa knew every entrance, every exit. Her go bag was packed and easily reachable by the door. She had cash in it, clothes, non-perishable foods, a box of hair dye, and a kitchen knife. She had a go bag stashed in her locker at work too. Her passport was easily accessible in a locked safety box she had kept hidden in a false bottom in the drawer by the door.

Her front door used to have a million locks that she had to manually put in place and although it helped to pretend that she felt safe. It was an illusion.

But in this new apartment, with all of Oli's fancy security features, Nessa had to relearn how to feel safe. She had to learn where things were in the apartment, so she had an escape route. The fact that there was only one entrance and exit scared her. If Gavin ever got in and barred the exit, she would have to go through him to get out.

Nessa had never been very technical, but she had paid attention when Oli and his security guy were showing her the front door lock, had set up the camera feeds to her tablet and phone, and when Oli had shown her the panic button hidden as a switch on the wall, Nessa had looked at Oli.

The rockstar had offered her a small smile. "Before you ask, Niamh hasn't told me anything. I swear. We had a conversation once if you remember, and you told me that Brian reminded you of a predator. I kinda came to the conclusion that someone hurt you. Niamh calls you family, so that means you're my family too, now. I look after my family."

Nessa had known then that Oli Scott was a good man, that he would be a great father and maybe husband to Niamh. She normally spent time assessing men to gauge how dangerous they were. Oli was safe. The Rebel Ink crew were safe. Darren was safe.

No, that was wrong.

Darren had the ability to tear down all of her carefully erected walls. He had the ability to make her think that maybe it wouldn't be a bad thing to let him take her to breakfast, with his cheeky grin and warm blue eyes, it would be so tempting to think that she was a normal woman who had the freedom to explore her attraction to Darren.

"I stayed away because I didn't want to be the reason why you were freaked out."

Gavin would never have said that. Nessa knew that Darren and Gavin were polar opposites. That Darren would not want to be the cause of her distress, while Gavin had relished it, fed on it.

Nessa got ready for work that night, spending a little extra time picking out her work clothes on the off-chance Darren would stop by. It had been four nights since he had helped her move her stuff into the apartment and he hadn't stopped by. She had been annoyed at herself for getting annoyed when he hadn't shown up.

It made her feel stupid and weak.

"Window dressing is all you are, Ness. Arm candy for me. A pretty, pretty airhead. Being stupid makes you more fuckable."

Nessa lifted her gaze and looked at herself in the mirror. After all she had been through, Nessa found it had to look at herself for too long. When she did, Nessa was reminded of the girl she had been, who exploited her good looks and caught the attention of a man who would one day try and kill her.

She looked at herself now, and her heart began to race. Her lipstick was far more subtle than what she had worn as a teenager, everything was more subtle. Panic flared in her chest and Nessa grabbed a makeup wipe and took off all the makeup on her face.

Who was she kidding?

She had no right to tart herself up and pretend like she was free to flirt and be carefree.

Nessa did not want to bring her messed up life into Darren's, especially when he was grieving the loss of his Gran. It was probably for the best that Darren had decided not to turn up the past few nights. Hopefully, he had realized that Nessa was not worth the hassle and was now gonna stay well clear.

But if it was for the best, then why did Nessa's stomach sink at the thought?

Shaking the thoughts from her head, Nessa grabbed her phone and her keys, made sure all the windows were locked, then set the code on the door before she stepped out and went down the stairs. When Nessa got to the bottom step, a little flutter of panic. Rushing back up the stairs, Nessa double-checked to make sure she had locked the door before heading back down again.

The best thing about the apartment was that she didn't even have to go outside to get into the book-shop. There was a side door that she could unlock with a code, a code that Niamh and Oli, Cliona, and Sorcha had. It made it easier to slip in and out of her new apartment.

The journey to behind the door when Gavin was free to go outside was shorter now.

Nessa walked into Rebel Books, and headed straight to the counter where Cliona was perched behind it. Her friend grinned at her, a little bit of mischief dancing in Cliona's eyes.

"Why do I feel like I should walk back out of here?"

Cliona slipped off her chair, still smiling as she said. "Oh hell no. Dani is back from London and we are gonna just hang out at home. And besides, you have plans too so I'm gonna go," Cliona stopped to rest a hand on Nessa's arm for a second. "Forget the past, forget the future. Just live in the moment, Nessa. I'll talk to you later."

Nessa must have looked confused because Cliona gave her a little nudge and Nessa turned and glanced up toward the upper floor of the shop, her breath catching.

Darren gave her a little wave from where he was sat at his usual table. He looked quite handsome, dressed in dark jeans, a plain tee, and a shirt thrown on over it. The sleeves were rolled up to his elbows, giving just a hint of the artwork etched into his skin.

When Nessa blinked, Cliona was already gone, and she had started to head toward Darren. She glanced at the table, expecting to see all his sketch-books, but instead, he had an array of Chinese food set out on the table, along with bottles of Lucozade, which Nessa was beginning to think was his fave drink.

Nessa told herself that the flutter in her stomach was nerves and not butterflies.

"What's all this?" she asked as she came to a stop by the table, and noted that Darren had managed to bring some of her fave dishes.

Darren shrugged his shoulders, and while he was trying not to smile, Nessa could see the corners of his mouth lifting. "I'm not a stalker or anything, but I called Oli and he asked Niamh, and she told me what you liked. If it's too much, I can go. No hassle."

Nessa felt her heart skip a beat. Darren was being so thoughtful, while not putting any pressure on her. He had gone to so much trouble, and she wasn't going to leave him thinking he had messed up when he was being so nice.

Lowering herself into the seat that gave her the best view of the door, Nessa glanced up at Darren. "You can't expect me to eat all of that on my own now, can you? I don't even think we can both finish all of that."

Darren grinned then, and it made his eyes seem even brighter. "That sounds awfully like a challenge. Do you know when I first started working at Rebel Ink, our old boss, before Hoggy took over, put a child lock on the fridge when he realized how much I could eat? My Gran used to say that it was because I never stopped, I had to burn lots of calories."

Nessa looked at Darren's body, then flushed and reached for the Lucozade in the hopes that Darren didn't notice. "I think it's something I'm gonna need to see to believe."

Awareness prickled at Nessa's nape and she turned to look at the window, thought she saw a shadow in the edge of the window and her heart began to race.

"Nessa?"

Nessa dragged her eyes from the window and gave Darren a warm smile. She was just imagining it... imagining a shadow staring at her through the glass. That's what she told herself anyways.

CHAPTER NINE

Nessa

NESSA SMILED for like the millionth time since her dinner with Darren on Wednesday night. After her initial trepidations, the easygoing nature of Darren put her at ease. They talked about art and music, and Nessa listened as Darren told her all about his Rebel Ink family. And that's exactly what he had called them, his family.

It had surprised Nessa, but then again, over the last two years, the women who worked and ran Rebel Books had become more and more like family to Nessa. She hadn't spoken to her own family in two years, not since she contacted them from the hospital, beaten half to death and her mother had told her that Nessa had made her bed, now she had to deal with the consequences.

Somehow, that flippant remark had hurt more than any blow Gavin could deliver.

But the other night, and the nights that followed, Nessa had enjoyed Darren's company and laughed and smiled more than she had in the longest time. Nessa knew that Darren was hurting, and avoiding his own grief, but he took the time to make her smile, to have her laugh.

When Nessa had told him that she was going to get a few hours of sleep and then go down the road to Cliona and Danika's for lunch, Darren had asked her what time. Nessa was always terrified to go outside during the day, when the chances of Gavin showing up to terrify her grew exponentially. It wasn't until Darren had asked her what time she was heading to Cliona's did Nessa remember that there would be about a thousand steps between Rebel Books and her destination.

A thousand steps where Gavin could be lurking and Nessa would be tempted to turn back and cancel. But she had already cancelled on Cliona before. Nessa didn't want to let her fears be the reason why she couldn't walk a thousand steps in the daylight.

Darren must have sensed her unease, because he told her that he had a client from ten in the morning, would be done by one for lunch and he'd be dying to stretch his legs before his tattoo at two. Nessa had nearly bitten his hand off when he offered.

At exactly one, Nessa went down the stairs and

opened the front door, glancing outside to see Darren already leaning against the wall. That cheeky grin of his deepened when he saw her, and as he pushed off the wall, Nessa allowed herself a moment to roam her eyes over him.

Darren was wearing shorts and a sleeveless black tee that had a Black Sabbath logo on it. Nessa could see the ink on his skin, her fingers itched to touch it. He looked good...he looked really good.

As they walked, Darren told her all about his client, and then tattoos he had planned for later today. Nessa kept looking over at him. His blue eyes seemed to dance with mischief when he looked at her at the exact moment, she looked at him. Nessa felt her cheeks heat as she looked away, and when Darren spoke again, there was a smile in his voice.

"I have one of your new artworks almost ready."

As they reached the door leading to the reception of the apartments where Cliona lived, Nessa stopped and turned to face Darren. "Why didn't you show me last night?"

That cheeky grin made her stomach dip.

"Then how would I be able to keep ya hanging out with me? You're only interested in my artwork."

No, there was a hell of a lot more than just artwork that drew her to Darren Fitzgerald.

When he looked at her face, he laughed, possibly misreading it as her trying to come up with something kind to say to him, to make him see that Nessa wasn't just using him for his artwork.

"I was only messing, Nessa," Darren told her as he reached out a tucked a strand of hair behind her ear and Nessa dared not breathe. "It's the Haribo that makes ya keep me around, right?"

Nessa let loose a chortle of laughter as she heard someone call Darren, stepped back as he glanced over his shoulder to where Cathal had hollered his name.

Darren grinned, winked, and then jogged away without another word.

Nessa was still smiling as she went inside, knocked on Cliona's door, and went inside. Cliona showed her around the apartment after telling Nessa that Danika was at the studio with Oli, working on music. She had never seen Cliona look so damn happy.

Sitting down on the couch, Nessa drank her coffee, while picking at the food that Cliona had put out for them. Nessa glanced at the bowl of jellies and couldn't stop the grin that curved her lips.

"I don't think I've ever seen you smile like that."

Nessa blinked and looked over at Cliona before she admitted. "It's been so long that I thought I'd forgotten."

Cliona grinned, then rested her chin on her knees. "So...Darren?"

Nessa took a sip of her tea. "What about him?"

"Have you two gotten naked yet or are ye still in the I'm pretending to be friends' mode?"

"Cliona!"

The other woman just wiggled her eyebrows at Nessa, reached over for a biscuit, and dipped it into her tea. "I mean, he's not my cup of tea but I can see the attraction. Anytime he's hung out with the gang, Darren's always the first one to get the party going. He's great craic."

"He's been very kind to me." Was all that Nessa said, but it was said in a tone that had Cliona tilting her head.

"Yano," Cliona started, setting her mug down on the table. "Before Danika, I'd never even believed in finding someone who knew all the parts of you and still loved you enough to stick around. But being with Danika has been the whirlwind of believing that I was worthy of her love."

This conversation had gotten intense really fast, and Nessa sat up a little straighter. Maybe she was being unfair to Darren by letting whatever the hell was between them continue on, when Nessa was not sure that she could ever truly let someone into her life in the ways that she had before, ways that had taken so much from her.

"I can see you thinking too hard, Ness," Cliona remarked, but her friend was still smiling. "But it is still okay to move on when someone has hurt you so much. Look at Niamh. I never, ever thought I would ever see the woman I knew again after what Brian did to her. But it took a rockstar to make her happy. Oli fits her like Danika fits me. Maybe Darren is the right man to fit you."

It had never been something that Nessa had even considered after everything that happened. Every day was a survival instinct. It was this awareness in Nessa that at any moment, the life she had built could be taken away from her. That Gavin would make good on his promise to her, the night he had almost killed her.

A hand in her hair, Gavin yanked her head up. "If you survive, I will never leave you. I will always be watching you, Nessa. And if you ever dare look at another man, I will gut him in front of you. You are mine, Nessa. Mine."

"Hey, no thinking of assholes."

Nessa blinked and gave Cliona a small smile. "Sorry."

Cliona reached over and took Nessa's hand. "You never, ever have to apologise to me. And I'm sorry if being nosy had brought up old wounds. But Nessa, that prick wins if you stop yourself from being happy. It gives him a power over you that he doesn't deserve. He tried to dim your shine and he fucking failed. Maybe it's not Darren, maybe it's someone else."

Nessa swallowed hard, and lifted her eyes to see Cliona watching her. There was no pity in her friend's eyes, just a fierceness that Nessa wished that she possessed herself. She wished that she wasn't as damaged as she was. She wished that Gavin didn't have this hold on her.

"You are mine, Nessa. Mine."

"But maybe some naked fun with Darren will help to heal things. Or maybe the orgasms will."

"Cliona!"

The door to the apartment opened and in strutted Danika Keane. She wore a Rebel Books tee, leggings, and a short camo jacket that was frayed at the edges. However, Nessa noticed the look of love in her eyes when she looked at Cliona.

"Hey babe, hey Nessa. What I miss?"

Danika came over and leaned down for a kiss, and Nessa looked away to give them some privacy, even though she was smiling.

"I was just telling Nessa it might be a good idea to let Fitz get her naked."

"Cliona!" Nessa exclaimed, but Danika was laughing.

Nessa must have looked so scandalized that the other two women laughed, and then Nessa was laughing and her heart, it felt a little lighter.

CHAPTER TEN

Darren

DARREN WAS GRINNING like an idiot all afternoon. He knew that someone had hurt Nessa, but making her smile, making her laugh, that was a priceless fucking feeling. He was used to everyone not taking him seriously, he was the joker of their dysfunctional family, and wanted to make everyone laugh in an attempt to mask the insecurities that he felt.

But something deep inside of him wanted Nessa to take him seriously. He wanted her to know that he was solid, that he was worth having around. That maybe, just maybe, he was worthy of her love.

Darren knew he was getting ahead of himself, and yet, stressing over Nessa meant he wasn't thinking about his grief and everything else in between. His cousin Eve had texted him earlier in the week to tell

Darren that his parents had asked if Eve knew if Darren had found a new place to live yet.

The reading of his Gran's will had taken place that day, and as he already knew she had left him the house. His parents, who had only appeared on video link, told the solicitor that they would be contesting the will. This wasn't news to Darren. They'd told him as much when they were at the wake, but hearing again felt like another kick in the gut.

And yet, Darren still couldn't go home.

Maybe they were right, his parents. Maybe the house should be sold and he'd just have to find somewhere else to live. Darren had some savings. Not enough to buy a house or anything but maybe get him somewhere to rent until his Gran's sold and he had a deposit. He didn't think that the house would feel the same now with just him taking up space.

Because the person who was the heart of the home was gone.

Darren had told his classmates when he was in primary school that his parents were dead. It was easier than explaining to the other boys that his parents didn't want him. He had mostly gotten away with it, but when he was in his first year in secondary school, his Da had shown up halfway through the day, after his Gran had a fall.

Neither he nor his Gran had known they were even in Ireland.

Darren was doodling on the back of his notebook

when the door to the classroom opened and one of the school secretaries came over to the teacher, said something, and then their eyes fell on him.

"Darren, your father is here to collect you."

Looking over at the other Darren in his class, who had risen to his feet already, Darren went back to his doodling when the teacher spoke again. "No, Darren Fitzgerald, your father is here to get you."

Mikey Lane turned round and looked at him. "I thought you said your Da was dead!"

"To me he is," Darren mumbled as he gathered up his stuff and headed out the door, where his father lingered in a suit that cost more than all the clothes in Darren's wardrobe combined.

"What are you doing here?" Darren asked him, and he heard the annoyance in his own tone.

"Let's go." That was all Diarmuid Fitzgerald said as he began to walk away.

Darren stayed where he was, just glanced at the secretary who was still hoovering by the door to the classroom, as if she would ask him if he wanted to go with his Da.

His Da glanced over his shoulder, and huffed out a breath that told Darren that his Da was not impressed by his impertinence before he voiced it.

"We do not have time for this Darren. Your grandmother had a fall and sprained her ankle. I need you to come home to look after her. I need to make my flight later tonight."

Darren ignored his Da as he hurried out the door, not wanting to get in the car with him, but it was the quickest way to get home to his Gran. When they arrived at the house, Darren expected his Da to come inside too, but he just tapped his hand on the steering wheel impatiently as his Ma came out the door.

Getting out of the passenger seat without another word to his Da, his Ma barely spared him a glance as she brushed past him to get into the car. Then his parents were gone and that pang in his chest ached so hard that Darren felt tears well in his eyes.

But he wasn't gonna cry. He wouldn't give um the satisfaction.

Pushing the thoughts of his parents out of his mind, Darren went inside to make sure Constance hadn't done anything to upset his Gran. Dropping his bag just inside the door, Darren kicked off his trainers, and then called out.

"Gran, it's Darren, where are ya?"

"I'm in the front room, Darren."

Heading in, Darren stopped and looked at his Gran. She was sat on her chair, with her leg on the pouf footstool, her right foot bandaged. He'd never seen his Gran injured like this. He'd nursed her when she'd had a bad chest infection, but his Gran had always seemed invincible. Darren didn't like how frail she looked.

His Gran must have noted the expression on Darren's face because she smiled. "I'm grand lad. Nothing a day or two in front of the telly won't solve.

Stupid old bat that I am, fell over trying to reach something on a shelf in the supermarket."

Darren was about to protest, to tell his Gran that she should have waited until he could have gone to the shops with her, but his Gran reached over and held out her mug to Darren.

"Be a good lad and make me a proper cup of tea. I was surprised Constance even knew how to switch on the kettle but she couldn't make a proper cuppa. The one she made me earlier was as weak as piss. And then come sit with me and we can watch some telly."

Darren blinked away the memories as he went about cleaning up his tattoo space. The two pieces he'd done today had been quick and easy, and he wanted to get tidied up so he could spend a couple of hours working on the artwork for Nessa.

Nessa had told him she liked gothic art, or art that meant something more than you'd expect. That had got him thinking, and while he didn't know what had happened to Nessa, he knew that it had affected Nessa in a major way. When he considered the sketch that had spoken to Nessa, he wanted to create something that spoke to her again.

The other day as he walked from the breakfast café to work, he saw an old antique birdcage in the window of an antiquities shop that Darren thought looked cool. That had given him the idea of the piece he was working on.

Darren was keeping with the black and grey theme

for this one too. He'd looked at other bird cages and used those as a reference. But then he'd drawn the outline of the cage with bent bars, and the door of the cage was open, and the lock was broken. The only thing Darren was trying to decide if he wanted to put a bird inside the cage, or just leave it open for interpretation.

He wanted to believe that the damage to the cage was done because the bird had fought so hard to be free.

A rap of knuckles against the wood of the door-frame dragged Darren from his thoughts, and Darren lifted his eyes to see Isaac standing in the doorway.

"There's some dude in a suit to see ya, Darren."

Rising to his feet, Darren walked out of his tattoo room, and down the hallway to where the dude in a suit was standing, looking around the place like he was afraid he might catch something if he touched anything.

"Can I help you?" Darren asked, and then the man checked that he was Darren before he handed him a brown envelope.

"Mr. Fitzgerald, I'm working on behalf of my clients to serve you with intention to contest a will. Please read over the contents of the letter, and I would strongly advise you to consult your own legal counsel. I'm sure that you would qualify for free legal aid."

Darren felt the blood in his veins heat as he took a meaningful step toward the solicitor, and he saw the suit cringe backwards. Isaac blocked Darren from advancing on the suit probably to avoid Darren being dragged up on an assault charge which wouldn't help his case.

"Tell my parents to have at it. You can fuck right off you pretentious prick. I'll see them in court."

The suit made a hasty exit, and all Darren wanted to do was to punch something, anything, and get this fucking anger out of him. He dragged his hands through his hair, and snarled as Isaac asked him if he was alright.

No...he was very fucking far from all right.

Darren hated feeling like this, feeling his grief and his pain all at once. He needed a drink. He needed to just not think or feel for a while.

CHAPTER ELEVEN

Darren

DARREN OPENED his eyes at the sound of the bin lorry coming to collect the rubbish from the side of Rebel Ink. The sun burned his eyes, and his head was absolutely pounding. His mouth felt like sandpaper, and he was gasping for something to drink.

Damn, he'd gone hard since leaving Rebel Ink on Saturday, and ended up asleep in his car. If the time on his phone was right, then it was around eleven and he was fucking late for work. He had like twelve missed calls from Cathal, Shay, and Isaac. He had a long day of tattooing ahead and he was not in the right headspace to deal with anything today.

He felt like a right muppet letting his parents still get to him after all this time. He told himself time and time again that he was better off without them, and that was fine. But it was when they went out of their way to *show* him just how little they cared about him that felt like a kick in the teeth all over again.

His Gran was dead. They had no reason now to be in his life. They had money and homes and all that...so why the hell were they so venomously trying to take the only home he had ever known right from under him? His parents would probably win, because they had money and could hire someone who would twist and pull and take what little Darren had left of the only person who had given a shit about him.

If it hadn't been for his Gran's love, then he might have ended up like Cathal...in foster homes and then on the streets. Cathal didn't talk much about the things he lived through, but his friend had some odd quirks that told Darren that his life hadn't been easy.

And Darren knew that it was just a house. It was just bricks and mortar. It didn't matter if he lived there, or in a cardboard box. His Gran would be with him wherever he was. And yet, he knew that his Gran would go mad if she knew what Constance and Diarmuid were planning on doing.

Leaning forward in the car, Darren reached over to the passenger seat and grasped the half-empty bottle of vodka. He knew he'd never get through the day sober so he unscrewed the cap and drank as much as he could stomach without puking it back up.

His phone rang again, and Darren silenced it as he got out of the car, vodka in hand, and headed toward

Rebel Ink. Shoving open the door, the beat of the music made his head throb even more. His vision blurred and he swayed slightly, nausea threatening to claw its way up his throat.

"Uncle Darren, are you okay?"

Fuck, Darren had forgotten that MJ had a day off today due to teacher training. He turned to look over at the Issacs's daughter and gave her a lopsided smile. "MJ! I'm grand. Just woke up late."

The little girl narrowed her gaze. "I think I'll call my dad."

Darren was about to tell MJ that there was no need to call Isaac when he heard a voice say. "MJ, head on back to the kitchen and grab some snacks. I hid the nice things in behind the porridge so they wouldn't get eaten. Shay's in there."

Closing his eyes, Darren waited for a few seconds before he pried his eyes open and turned back around. Cathal stood in the archway that led back to the tattoo rooms, a frown on his face, and his arms folded across his chest. He glanced down at the bottle of vodka, then back to Darren and you could almost feel the disappointment.

Setting the bottle on the counter, Darren leaned against the counter and tried to stop the turbulent thoughts running through his brain.

"I'll grab a quick shower and I'll be good to go." He said, but still didn't move from where he stood.

"You need to go home and sober up, Darren. I can smell the cheap vodka sweating from your pores."

Darren heard the judgement in Cathal's tone, and it hit him more than he would have liked. Another fucking person who was disappointed in him, and he was just so sick of being the fuck up that everyone laughed at.

"Is the great Cathal Horgan disappointed in me?" Darren sniggered, scrubbing a hand down his face. "Ya, well get in line behind everyone else."

"Go home, Darren," Cathal said through gritted teeth.

"I fucking can't!" Darren yelled and pushed away from the counter, ignoring how the room spun. "I can't go inside that fucking house cos she's not there anymore, and they want to take it from me anyways so how the hell can I go back? How the fucking hell can I go back?"

His voice had risen as he spoke, until the last few words were all but screamed at Cathal. His friend's expression didn't even change, and the calm look just made Darren angrier. His hands coiled into fists and Darren wanted to get all the pain, the anger, the sadness out of him and to do that all he could do was hurt himself.

"Go and sober up. Come back when you have a hold of yourself. If you don't want to go home, go upstairs and shower, eat something, and then we can talk."

Darren laughed, the dark tone sounding foreign to him. "Yano what, Hoggy, go fuck yourself. I lived me whole fucking life without a Da. I didn't need one then, and I certainly don't need ya to start acting like one now."

Cathal stared at him, as Shay and Isaac came out from the back. Isaac had a confused look on his face as he said. "Can we just take it down a notch? MJ's scared."

And of course that made Darren feel like a grade A prick. He loved MJ. He never wanted her to be afraid of him.

"Darren is gonna go and sober up and then we can have a more civilized talk when he's more himself."

When he was more himself?

So when he went back to being the goofball? To being the first person to get the party started or the first to get up to mischief? Was that all he was to them all? The screw-up, the stupid idiot they kept around for shits and giggles.

Darren felt like his chest was about to explode and he just couldn't deal with this crap. Rummaging into the pocket of his, Darren took out his keys. He fumbled with the front door key to Rebel Ink, then with what felt like a hand around his throat, set the key down on the counter.

Shay tried to push past Cathal, but he wouldn't budge. just stared at Darren, the only inclination that he was feeling anything at all was the muscle that ticked in his jaw.

"Darren..." Shay started to say, but Darren shook his head, blood pounding in his ears.

"I'll always be just a fucking joke to you lot, won't I? The screw-up, the joker, the unfucking reliable guy who's just thick and useless. But hey, he can tattoo, and he's good for a laugh, so let's keep him around."

Cathal's features softened and Darren didn't want that. He wanted Cathal to force his hand, to make this easier on him.

"I get it, okay. You guys have never been that close with me and I get it now. So I'm done. I'm gonna bounce. I'll come back for my shit another day."

Jerking away from the counter, Darren staggered toward the door as he heard Isaac say. "Is that what you really feel, Fitz? This is our family."

Darren looked over his shoulder, then shrugged. "Does it really matter? If anyone should know when they're not wanted, it's me. I'm tired of being the butt of all the jokes. I'm tired of being the idiot you guys hide in cars to avoid. I'm just sick and tired of constantly searching for everyone's goddamn approval."

His voice cracked and he blinked away the hot furious tears that threatened to leak from his eyes. Jaysus Christ the last thing he needed for his goddamn self-esteem was to bawl like a baby in front of everyone.

"Are ya just gonna let him walk out Cathal?

Fucking do something." Shay urged Cathal but Darren was already halfway out the door before Cathal finally spoke.

"I'm sure when Darren has sobered up, he will come back."

And there it was. Cathal knew he had no one left. That it was expected for him to crawl back with his head hanging and fucking apologise, beg to be taken back. But Darren was done with begging for the love of those around him. He was done covering up just how much he craved being wanted.

"I do not have the capacity in me to love him, Annie. Neither does Diarmuid. That is why we didn't want him."

Striding forward, he grabbed the vodka bottle, slugged it even though his stomach rolled, and headed right on out the door without a second glance.

CHAPTER TWELVE

Nessa

NESSA HAD TRIED to get some sleep before her shift that evening, but she had spent hours tossing and turning. Cliona's words the other day had Nessa thinking hard. She wasn't about to deny her feelings for Darren had taken her by surprise, because she never expected to feel desire again after what happened to her. And yet, Darren had somehow charmed his way past her defenses.

Would it be so bad to give in to her attraction and find a way through her trauma?

Walking over to the window, Nessa hugged herself as she looked out onto the street, her eyes scanning the road before they landed on the storefront of Rebel Ink. There was this little part of her, the old Nessa, who had the confidence and would have walked right across the road, strode into Rebel Ink, and asked Darren out for a drink.

But the Nessa she was now was utterly terrified. The thought of going outside during the day threatened to drown her in panic, her chest tight even at the very suggestion. She despised the fact Gavin still had this hold on her. Hated that she was still giving him that power. But faced with the prospect that Nessa might run into Gavin if she dared venture out in the day, that fear would always triumph.

Movement caught her eye as the door to Rebel Ink opened and Darren staggered out, with what looked like a bottle of alcohol in his grasp. He stumbled into the road, and Nessa clasped a hand over her mouth as a car ground to a halt seconds before it would have hit him.

What the hell was going on?

Darren slapped the bonnet of the car, then stepped back and the car drove off. Cathal came out the door, as did the shop's manager Shay Gleeson. Shay said something that had Darren taking a drink from the bottle, only to realize that it was empty and he threw it at the wall of Rebel Ink.

Nessa heard Cathal swear, then tell Darren to come back inside.

Darren laughed, and then he yelled. "Stop trying to be my fucking dad!"

Pain. That was what she heard in his voice. She knew what pain like that felt like. Buried behind the sure smile, and easy laughter, was a human being who was in pain and this was his way of hurting himself even more.

Cathal reached for Darren, and he jerked backward, tangling his legs and landing hard in the middle of the road. Nessa's heart was in her throat as Darren just lay there, with Shay calling his name.

She should go to him, right? She should go and help her friend?

In the span of a few seconds, Nessa ran through every possible scenario of what could happen if she went outside. Anxiety pooled in her stomach as she watched Darren sit up, still in the middle of the road, and Nessa could see he looked defeated, beaten down, and hopeless.

Nessa moved before she had a chance to let the panic consume her. She keyed in the code on the security panel near the door that Oli had his people install, and rushed down the stairs, using the private side door to step out into the street.

The midmorning sun warmed her skin, and Nessa froze, rooted to the spot as her gaze darted from side to side as if she was expecting Gavin to leap out of any corner and strike her. She had already been outside now for almost 90 seconds and her chest felt like it was gonna explode.

"Darren! Get out of the fucking road before you get yourself killed, ya idiot!"

Shay's worried tone snapped Nessa from her panic.

She checked to make sure there were no cars coming before she jogged across the road, ignoring the pointed stares from Cathal and Shay as she crouched down in front of Darren.

His eyes were glazed and they were on the verge of tears. Nessa could see clearly that whatever had happened to him had taken the spark of life out of him and left behind a man who was hurting himself. He stared at Nessa like he didn't notice that Nessa was right in front of him.

The smell of alcohol almost triggered her, but she told herself that Gavin drank beer and not spirits. That Darren was not the same as Gavin, not by a long shot.

Reaching out, Nessa noted that her hand was shaking before she gently put it on Darren's chest. "Hey, it's me, Nessa. How about we move out of the road and go somewhere a little less likely to get us both knocked down?"

Darren didn't react at all, just looked at her with dead eyes. Shit, this was really bad wasn't it?

Taking a deep breath, Nessa moved her hand to cup his cheek. The moment she touched his face, Darren blinked and focused. "Nessa? What's going on?"

Offering him a small smile, Nessa made a feeble attempt at a joke. "Well, you looked like you were having a great time playing chicken with cars that I thought I'd join you."

Darren blinked again, then glanced around,

putting a hand to his temple. "I'm so fucking tired, Nessa."

Nessa knew the feeling.

Taking her hand away from his cheek, Nessa got to her feet. "I know. How about you come back to mine and get some sleep?" Then a little louder so that Cathal and Shay heard her, hoping Darren's family would understand. "I bet it's hard to get a good night's sleep in your car and with the nights you've been spending at Rebel Books."

"Okay."

Darren got to his feet then, turned away from them all, and started to head toward the bookshop and her apartment. It suddenly dawned on her that she would be alone, with Darren, in her apartment. It was both thrilling and terrifying at the same time.

"Has he really been sleeping in his car? Why didn't he come to us?"

Nessa kept her eyes on Darren as she replied to Cathal's question. "Because he felt stupid about it. He felt ashamed that he couldn't go home and I think he was afraid that people would think he was an idiot."

Cathal didn't say anything in response, but Nessa could tell that he was surprised. Shay touched his arm, gave Nessa a smile and they headed back inside Rebel Ink. Nessa shifted her gaze to where Darren leaned against the doorway and then back at Cathal.

"You don't have to look after him. I can bring him to mine and make sure he gets some sleep."

Nessa shook her head. "I'm not sure what went down but maybe a break would be good. We've...we've become friends lately."

Cathal quirked a brow, but didn't comment on what Nessa had said. "Fitz sleeps like the dead the moment his head hits the pillow. I'll come over later to check on him."

Nessa nodded, then headed back across the road when she heard Cathal say her name, and when she glanced back at him, Cathal just said, "Thank you for looking out for my brother."

Her cheeks flushed as she headed to Darren. They didn't speak as they went up the stairs, and Darren didn't pass any comment on how Nessa locked the door, bolted it, and then checked that the door leading to Rebel Books was locked too.

Darren didn't say anything either after they stepped inside the apartment and Nessa put in the code to lock the doors, both in her apartment, and down the end of the stairs. She guided him over to the couch, and he sat down, and Nessa sat down beside him.

He said nothing for a few minutes and then it was like the words needed to come out, in order for Darren to begin to heal. The tears he'd been holding back finally slid down his face as he muttered. "Why couldn't they love me? Why didn't they want me, Nessa? What's wrong with me?"

Nessa didn't know who he was talking about, but

then Darren began to sob, the sound heart-breaking and painful as Darren put his hands to his face, his shoulders shaking as he tried to hold back his tears, but the dam had been broken, and there was no putting halt to it now.

She wrapped her arms around Darren, and felt the wetness of his tears on her t-shirt as she told him that there was nothing wrong with him, nothing at all. Darren shifted, laying his head down on her lap, and Nessa ran her fingers through his hair. She let him lay there, until he had cried himself out, and into a deep sleep.

Nessa's heart was pounding. She kept stroking Darren's hair, the weight of his head on her lap the closest that Nessa had been with a man in a long time. There was no denying that something was happening between them, but with everything that he was dealing with and Nessa's trauma, was there any hope for them?

Or would she be another person that Darren would find himself asking – what is wrong with me?

CHAPTER THIRTEEN

Darren

DARREN PEELED OPEN his eyes and wished he hadn't. The morning wasn't exactly bright but his head was throbbing and his stomach felt like he'd been kicked square in the gut. Memories of what happened yesterday flashed in his mind before he groaned and tried to sit up.

The entire room spun.

"There's coffee on the table if you can stomach it."

Darren jerked his head round to see Nessa standing in the kitchen, a mug in her own hands as she offered him a small smile. Jesus, he'd made an utter eejit of himself for bawling like a baby with Nessa, and any kind of romantic aspirations that Darren might have had been washed away the moment he'd started crying.

Putting his head in his hand to try and hide his

embarrassment, Darren heard Nessa come toward him, and then he felt her hand on his knee, so he lifted his gaze to look into her green eyes. He opened his mouth to apologise for what happened last night, but Nessa smiled, and he damn well forgot what he wanted to say.

"How long was I out?" He asked instead, his voice thick.

"A while," Nessa replied. "I went to work last night for a few hours until Cliona could come to cover me. Cathal was right, you sleep like the dead."

Darren rolled his eyes, and winced at how much it hurt. "I'm sorry."

Nessa glossed over his apology, and Darren was hyper-aware that her hand was still on his knee. "Cathal called over and stayed with you while I was at work. He's worried about you. He said to tell you that he covered your appointments for the next few days and your key is waiting when you feel up to it."

He'd been an ass to Cathal, and all because he had felt like he didn't deserve to have someone care about him like Cathal did. The insecurities he had were his, and he shouldn't have taken them out of his friend. Darren knew he would have to apologise for behaving like he had, even though Cathal would tell him that he didn't need any apologies: that they were family.

"So, since I'm not working tonight," Nessa began as she chewed on her bottom lip and Darren instantly had to fight the urge to lean forward and kiss her.

"Why don't you take a shower, get into some fresh clothes – Cathal dropped them over – and then if you feel up to it, me and you could go to your place."

His heart clenched but Darren tried to deflect from what he was feeling by saying. "Is that your nice way of telling me that I stink?"

Nessa lifted her hand off his knee and made a gesture with her fingers. "Just a tad."

Darren chuckled, as Nessa rose and went over to the kitchen, pointing out where the bathroom was and where his change of clothes was. Darren retreated to the bathroom, showering and changing as quickly as possible. When he was suitably clean and dressed, he opened the bathroom to the smell of rashers.

Nessa was just cutting a bacon sandwich in half, pushing the plate toward him. His stomach rumbled, as he leaned against the breakfast, before reaching for the sandwich. "You're defo heaven-sent."

Was that a faint blush on her cheeks?

Darren devoured the sandwich, and then drank the glass of OG Nessa poured for him. Once he had eaten, Darren picked up his plate and took his glass to the sink, but that put him and Nessa within touching distance.

"You don't have to do that." She argued, but Darren only grinned.

"You cooked, I clean. Fair is fair. Besides, me Gran would clip me round the ear if I didn't clean up after meself."

He winced when he heard himself refer to his Gran in the present, and not in the past tense. If Nessa noticed, she didn't say anything, just finished her cup of coffee, and smiled when Darren held out his hand to take it from her to rinse it out.

When he was done, Darren turned and angled his body toward Nessa. A wave of smugness coursed through him when Nessa's gaze dipped to take in his body. He cleared his throat, and she yanked her gaze back to his face, a flush of pink on her cheeks.

"Right, okay," Nessa said, taking a step back and putting some distance between them. "So...what do you think about us heading to your place?"

Darren closed his eyes. Was he really ready to face the only home he had ever known and feel how different that it was now that his Gran was gone? Was he being childish digging his heels in by not wanting to go back?

"I think it must be hard. But once you go there the first time, it will be so much easier."

Maybe Nessa was right, and it was like ripping off a band-aid. He just needed to get it over with.

Darren nodded his head, and just watched as Nessa did all these security things before they walked out of the apartment and headed to where Darren's car was parked. He wanted to ask her what had happened that she was so security conscious, but now really wasn't the time. They drove in relative silence, until Darren parked his car in the drive.

Before he lost his nerve, he got out, and glanced over his shoulder to make sure that Nessa was with him. Her face was a little pale and she looked around her as she hurried forward. Darren braced himself as he put the key in the door, pushed it open, and stepped back to let Nessa go in before him.

Nessa strode into the house, and Darren paused to pick up the post and set it on the side table. Following Nessa into the living room, he leaned in the doorway, trying to process his emotions, as Nessa wandered about and looked at all the framed photos on the wall.

"You look like such a happy child," Nessa remarked.

"I was to be fair. I knew my Gran loved me. I just thought that everyone grew up with their parents MIA."

Nessa picked up a photo of him and her eating ice cream by the beach. "She loved you. I can see it. You were lucky to have her. My parents were MIA as well. I would have loved to have had someone like your Gran to look out for me."

There was this sadness in Nessa's tone that made a part of Darren want to wrap his arms around her and chase it away. But he left her to explore a little while he went and did some tidying up. It gave him time to try and settle the storm of emotions inside of him. There were so many memories contained in the walls of this house, this home.

And while he had feared that being in here

knowing his Gran would never be here waiting for him when he came home again, being here allowed Darren to remember that it was in this house where he had learned what love truly meant, and his Gran wouldn't want him to be hurting himself like he had been.

Darren washed up the ware and set his Gran's mug in its rightful place beside his before he went back into the front room to where Nessa was sat on the couch. She looked up when he came in, and Darren saw her check her watch, and fidget with the ends of her shirt.

"Thank you for coming with me. Having ya here made it easier."

Nessa looked over to the array of photos. "You can feel the love in this house. It's in all the pictures, and in the artwork on the walls – it's exactly how a home should be."

Darren came over to sit down beside her, giving her space. "Was it not like that for you?"

Nessa shook her head. "My parents weren't around. I lived with them but they were hyper-focused on their careers. I rebelled a lot. I know now it was a cry for attention. On days when I'm really mad, I blame them for what happened after. For not caring enough to realise that the love and attention that I craved from them was a weakness for others to exploit."

Darren knew then that he was lucky to have had his Gran, because there had always been someone to love him. Nessa made it sound like there was no one to love her. That made Darren mad as hell because Nessa deserved to be loved.

He reached over and took her hand in his, and she looked at him, her eyes wide, and he saw the fear in them. Darren knew it wasn't of him, because she squeezed his hand. And as Nessa had been there for him last night, Darren, who wanted to know all her secrets, was content to wait for this beautiful woman to open up to him.

His heart kicked up a gear when Nessa scooted closer to him, their legs touching, the side of their bodies pressed against the others, and still Nessa kept on holding his hand.

CHAPTER FOURTEEN

Nessa

THERE WAS something comforting about being in this house, where love was given freely, with Darren's fingers entwined in hers that gave her the strength to share her story. It was a story that she hadn't even shared all of the details with her friends, just enough so that they understood why she was the way she was.

But with Darren, Nessa didn't want to have any secrets.

"I don't want to taint the warm and safe feeling that I have in your home with the ugliness of what happened to me. And I might not get through it. I've never told anyone all the details."

Darren lifted her hand to his lips, kissed her knuckles, her skin tingling even as her body heated. She knew that Darren found her attractive, but would he still feel that way after she revealed so much of herself? Being with her, living with all of her quirks? That, would not make her good girlfriend material.

"I don't want to tell you," Nessa whispered, but she knew Darren heard her, "Because I don't want you to see me differently when you know who I am."

"I already know who you are, Nessa. You are the girl who kept me company when I was trying to get used to being alone. You're the girl who held me all night and the girl who stopped me playing chicken with cars when being a drunken idiot."

Nessa laughed and it eased some of the tension in her chest. "I used to be the girl who got drunk and played chicken with cars. I used to be the girl everyone called to get the party started. I think she died when I met Gavin."

Swallowing hard, Nessa closed her eyes and counted to ten, trying to convince herself that Gavin couldn't harm her here, with Darren holding her hand. That in this house filled with love and memories, Nessa was safe.

"When I first met Gavin, I thought he was this white knight coming to save me from a life where I was unwanted, and unloved. He was older, and charming, and handsome, and he wanted me. I was flattered because even though I was young, he treated me like a woman and not a girl."

She glanced at Darren, hoping to gauge his reaction but he just had this look of calmness on his face, but oh, his eyes, in his eyes Nessa could see that he was angry, and from the gentle way in which he was holding her hand, his anger was not directed at her.

Nessa told Darren all about the things Gavin did to her over the course of their relationship, how he alienated her from her friends, and how she had tried to make him happy so that he would love her. How she'd moved in with him, and decided not to go to college to make Gavin happy. How slowly over time she lost herself in order to make sure she was the kind of girl Gavin wanted to keep around.

Nessa swallowed down her fear, all her instincts telling her that this would be the nail in any kind of romantic relationship with Darren. She could hear Gavin's voice clear as day in her head, telling her she was useless, that no one but him could ever love her.

"It's okay, Nessa. I'm here. I'm not going anywhere."

The relief that washed over her was enough to cause her to shiver, and while her story was far from over, Nessa knew that she had to get it out, even if she never told another soul all the gory details.

"Looking back, I wish I'd seen the signs. Gavin hid who he really was so fucking well. But he showed his true colours when I found out that his dad's business was a front for the fact that they were drug dealers. I hate drugs and I was so mad at him for not telling me the truth. I screamed at him that I was gonna leave him, that I didn't want to be in love with a drug-dealing scumbag."

Not wanting to see the look in Darren's eyes when she said the next part, Nessa looked away. "The first time that he hit me, it was just a split lip and a bruise on my cheek. He told me he was sorry and that I shouldn't have threatened to leave him. That he couldn't survive without me."

Darren squeezed her hand, but he didn't say anything. Nessa went on, telling Darren how Gavin started to take the drugs he was meant to be selling. That he drank more too. But it was when Nessa said that when he was high and drunk, that the beatings were usually worse, or he'd expect sex until he passed out, Darren couldn't keep quiet any longer..

"Fucking coward. Fucking coward hitting a woman. And that's not me being sexist because my cousin Eve is one of the baddest bitches on the planet and she takes punches for a living. You didn't sign up for that, Nessa. I could kill him."

Nessa looked at Darren, and her heart ached at how fierce his expression was, and she knew that he meant it. That Darren would protect her.

"Nessa, you know if you were coerced into having sex with him so that you would be safe, that's still rape right?"

She gave a slight incline of her head. "It was easier to take than his fist."

Darren wrapped his arms around her, pulled her to

him, and Nessa shuddered. Gods, how long had it been since she'd let anyone hold her? How long since she hadn't spent her days checking the time to make sure that she was indoors whenever there was a chance Gavin might be waiting to pounce on her.

She felt the brush of Darren's lips on the top of her head. "Please tell me the asshole is locked up in prison with some dudes who would be more than happy to make him their bitch."

Nessa barked out a laugh and untangled herself reluctantly from Darren. Feeling restless, Nessa got to her feet and walked over to the window, looking out as rain started to fall. "I wish I could tell you that Gavin got what was coming to him, but to understand what happened next, I need to tell you the worst of it."

Closing her eyes, Nessa could almost feel every strike again, could almost feel the blood leaving her body, her bones cracking under the force of Gavin's attack. But she was getting ahead of herself.

"I was with him for six years, and I couldn't see a way out. I fantasised about killing him because prison would be better than living in hell. He punched me in the face when I didn't cook his steak right, and I knew he'd kill me in the end, so I spiked Gavin's beer with antihistamines. They knocked him out. It was the closest I came to freedom."

"So, I started to make plans. I went on to a victim's chatroom and got a go bag ready. I saved up cash so he couldn't trace any cards I used, 'cause they were all linked to his accounts."

Nessa rubbed her arms, because while everything about what she endured was hard, knowing she almost died was the hardest thing Nessa could talk about, because she didn't want to admit to anyone that death would have been better than going back to Gavin.

"I was ready to go. All planned. He was away for a weekend, and I was gonna run. Then he found the antihistamines and fucking lost it. Ten minutes. Just six hundred seconds. That was all it took for him to almost beat me to death. He broke my ribs, and snapped my leg when I tried to crawl away. Then he hauled me by the hair to the bathroom to drown me."

She continued to talk; afraid she wouldn't get it all out. Nessa told Darren that when the guards got into the apartment, Gavin had her head under the water. That there was this lovely guard who stayed with her in the ambulance and kept her awake and when she woke up from surgery, he was there so that she wouldn't wake up alone.

"He came with me to court too," Nessa explained, blowing out a shaky breath. "I testified and the judge gave him a lenient sentence. A restraining order to stop him from coming near me, and a tag, and a curfew. That's why I work nights because I know he can't be out at night. Once his time is done though, he will come for me like he promised. Maybe even before that."

Nessa had always known that Gavin would not be content to see her out and living a life without him. He'd rather kill her and know that she was eternally his. All that Nessa had was borrowed time and she wanted to stop living in fear and soak in as much as possible before Gavin came for her.

And she wanted that with Darren

CHAPTER FIFTEEN

Darren

DARREN HAD ALWAYS THOUGHT himself more of a lover than a fighter, but in that moment, if the prick who had hurt Nessa was standing in front of him, Darren woulda loved to give him a dose of his own fucking medicine.

No wonder Nessa was so security-conscious. No wonder she worked nights and always seemed like she was afraid. She was afraid. She was terrified of a monster who had managed to evade justice and she was bricking it that he was gonna come for her again.

Over his dead body.

Darren didn't want to frighten her with how aggressively he wanted a face-to-face with this Gavin, because the last thing that Nessa needed was another man in her life who spoke with violence.

"Do ya know how strong you are?" Darren said, shelving his anger for the moment. Nessa flinched and didn't look at him, she just continued to stare out the window. He stayed where he was sitting and then said. "That prick didn't break you, Nessa. You are standing in my living room, being kind to me when I'm grieving, when now I know how much it cost you to be here. You are fucking amazing."

Nessa turned to him, and where Darren expected to see tears, all he saw was a determination in her green eyes. Her hand slid up to cup her neck, and Darren wanted to be the one holding her. She chewed on her bottom lip, her eyes still on him.

"I told myself when I woke up in that hospital room that I wouldn't let him win. That I would prove that I was better than him by living my life. But I'm still cowering in the corner waiting for the next blow. You know what's the one stupid thing that makes me hate myself even more?"

"What?"

"That he's still the last man I had sex with. That he was the last man inside me and until now, there hasn't been any man that I've wanted to get naked with."

Darren felt his body harden, and when Nessa licked her lips, Darren's pulse began to race.

"Nessa, you're gonna have to spell it out for me because right now, there is something other than my brain thinking for me and I don't want it to be wrong."

Nessa laughed then, a husky tone that felt like a stroke of his cock. She tentatively walked over to him, then straddled his lap, her hands clasping on the side of his neck, her core pressed against the rigidness of his erection, and it took all of Darren's restraint not to rock into her.

Her lips grazed his jaw, and Darren hissed out a breath, needing his hands on her.

"Nessa, can I touch you?"

She blinked down at him, like she was surprised he would ask her, but then she smiled, and Darren felt truly blessed that he was worthy of her smile, that she could still smile after all that she had been through. She nodded her head and Darren slid his hands down her back to cup her ass.

For a moment, he saw uncertainty in Nessa's eyes, like all her confidence had gone. Darren wasn't having any of that shit.

"Do you know that I have been fantasizing about having my hands on your ass since the first moment I saw you, and then you bent over and those jeans you like to wear hugged your curves. I had to stroke myself to erotic images of you in my head."

"Darren!"

He grinned as he gave that ass a squeeze. "Gods' honest truth. I've been lusting after you since then but I knew you were so out of my league that I didn't even try."

A blush tinged Nessa's cheeks. "I was in the shop

the day you did a strip tease for the media. I've had my own fantasies about licking every single tattoo etched on your skin."

Darren's cocked twitched and he groaned, pulling Nessa flush against him as she lowered her head down, her lips grazing his. The kiss started off slow, with little presses of lips, because Darren didn't want to rush things between them. But when Nessa used her teeth to nip at his bottom lip, Darren couldn't hold back.

Snaking one hand up and into her hair, Darren licked at the seam of Nessa's lips, and she opened for him. Darren licked his way into her mouth, stroking his tongue against hers. Nessa rocked against him, and they both moaned. The kiss deepened, with Nessa's arms around his neck, her nails scratching his skin and Darren wanted those nails in his back when he was inside her.

They kept kissing, with Nessa rocking against him and he made a strangled sound in the back of his throat. Nessa froze, her whole body going ridged. He was panting as he broke the kiss, and looked right into Nessa's eyes before he said. "You keep doing that and I'm gonna embarrass myself."

Nessa looked confused so he grinned. "If you keep that delicious friction up then I'm gonna come in my pants and I would much prefer to come inside you."

With a quick blink of her eyes, Nessa gave him a dazzling smile, then shimmied her body back a little, then popped the buttons on his jeans. Darren swore as he gently grasped Nessa's wrist, nudged her off his lap, and then got to his feet.

Nessa started to strip, and Darren stood there watching this fierce, beautiful woman taking off her clothes. Darren kicked off his own shoes, then his tee, a wave of male smugness making him feel like a right cocky shit as Nessa's eyes devoured him.

Darren cupped her face and kissed her, then took Nessa's hand and led her up the stairs to his bedroom. When he closed the door, Nessa sucked in a breath and Darren was worried it was too much too soon for her.

But Nessa didn't look afraid. No, she was looking at the murals painted on his walls of dragons, of heroes slaying monsters, of mythical beasts. She reached out to touch the wall. Darren came up behind her, swept her hair off her neck, then kissed the nape of her neck.

"I have other artwork you can admire. And it's all on my body."

Nessa chuckled, turning in his arms and then they were kissing again. Her hands roamed his body, and when she pushed him down on the bed so she could explore the ink on his skin, Darren gripped the sheets so that he wouldn't reach for her. This was for Nessa, for her to reclaim her sexuality and a part of herself that Gavin had taken from her.

But Darren only had so much patience and when she traced her tongue over the tattoo of a skull on his chest, her other hand sliding up so that her nail flicked his nipple, Darren knew he had to be inside her.

Rolling them so that Nessa was underneath him, Darren braced himself up on his elbows, looking down at Nessa.

"Is this okay?" He asked her, and she nodded.

"Gods, yes. Don't you dare stop."

Darren gave Nessa a wicked grin. Then he pressed a kiss in the space between her breasts, then trailed his lips down and down until Nessa sucked in a breath and Darren spread Nessa's legs a little wider before he licked his tongue up her wet core.

Fuck, he'd never tasted anything as good as Nessa before.

Nessa groaned and scraped her nails along his scalp as Darren plunged his tongue into her, then fucked her with his tongue. He heard her moans, and the rapidness of her breathing, and knew she was close, and then he slid a finger into her wet hot sheath and Nessa came apart, her body shuddering as Darren stroked her through it.

He gave one last languid lick before he rolled off Nessa, went to his dresser, and took out a box of condoms. Taking one from the box, he tossed it on his dresser, then stroked himself as Nessa watched, before he rolled on the condom.

Darren got back on the bed, and kissed Nessa as he positioned himself where his mouth had just been. His gaze locked it Nessa's, as she hooked one leg around his hip, her hands running up and down his spine. He waited, giving her time to process and it was him that laughed when Nessa growled and demanded that he fuck her right now.

He pushed into her slowly, pushing in and then pulling almost all the way out before going in again. Then Nessa scored his back, his control snapped, and he slid all the way in. Nessa dug her nails in harder, and Darren moved, slowly at first, then faster as Darren drank in the look of pleasure on Nessa's face as she came and watching her took Darren over the edge with her.

When they both could think again, Darren pulled out of Nessa, and discarded the condom, as Nessa went to the bathroom. Darren climbed into the bed, and Nessa came out and got in beside him, resting in the crook of his arm and when she fell asleep, Darren knew that he wanted to fall asleep with Nessa in his arms every goddamn night.

CHAPTER SIXTEEN

Nessa

NESSA WOKE and stretched in the bed; her body sated in a way that it hadn't been in a long time. Reaching over, she realized that Darren wasn't in the bed beside her, but she could hear him whistling to the radio downstairs. It was so cute that it made her smile.

Last night had been amazing. She could still feel Darren inside her and desire licked at her. it was strange to think that she had been with another man, that Gavin was no longer the last man to be with her. For the longest time, Nessa had been ashamed of her body, of how it might attract a man's attention, but Darren had treated her with respect even when she could tell that her body was something he craved.

She heard footsteps on the stairs, and with a wicked idea, she kicked off the sheets and just lay on the bed, naked. Darren strode in, two mugs in his hand, dressed only in a pair of boxers, and his eyes hungrily roamed over her body.

"I don't know whether to fuck you or draw you like that. All sexy and naked in my bed."

Nessa chuckled, rolling her eyes, but it was exactly what she wanted from him. "Alright Leo."

When Darren looked at her with a confused expression, Nessa explained. "It's from a movie. Kate Winslett is laying naked, and she asks Leo DiCaprio to draw her like he does French women."

When he still looked confused, Nessa laughed. "Oh my god, you've not seen Titanic?"

Darren set the mugs down on the bedside table and leaned down to kiss her.

"Oh that. Shay made me watch it a few years back. I fell asleep. She called me an uncultured fool. But maybe we need to watch it, if it means that you'll let me draw you naked. Or maybe I can draw you from memory because the very sexy look on your face when I gave you an orgasm is tattooed on my brain."

Nessa grabbed a pillow and smacked him with it. However, Darren just chortled with laughter throwing the pillow aside so that he could clamour onto the bed beside her. Resting one hand on his stomach, he reached for his mug to his lips, then grimaced.

"The coffee's black. There was no milk in the fridge. Hell, there wasn't anything edible in the fridge either, but I ordered some food and coffee that should be here in a while."

Nessa reached for her own coffee, took a sip, and then set it down. She watched Darren from the corner of her eye. His dark brown hair was sticking up all over the place, his lips were curved into a smile, and his fingers tapping on his taunt stomach. Nessa hadn't had the time last night to truly take in all of the ink that adorned his skin, but now, in the light of day, she could do so at her leisure.

Shifting so that she sat up in the bed, she took the coffee from his hands and set it on the table, her breasts brushing against his bare skin, and he sucked in a breath that had heat pooling between her legs.

Using her fingers, Nessa traced the tattoos that had been intricately woven into his flesh. She drew the outline of the skull on his chest, the spiders and moths that seemed to flutter down toward his navel. He had an Oni right on his ribs that Nessa knew must have hurt like hell. Nessa continued to drink every inch of him in, learning every tattoo, every piece of art, every expanse of his body.

It was quite clear that Darren was turned on by her exploration of his body, his cock straining for release in his boxers, the head poking out of the waistband. Thinking wicked, wicked thoughts, Nessa leaned down and pressed a kiss to the tiger tattoo that curled around Darren's navel.

The tip of his erection brushed against her chest

and Darren swore. Slipping her hand inside his boxers, Nessa wrapped her hand around his cock, and stroked the hot flesh in her hand. Then she leaned down and flicked her tongue over the slit.

"Fuck, Nessa...just fuck."

This was the kind of power that Nessa had lost in the six years with Gavin. The power to be sensual. To be sexual. To have a man want her like Darren did, to let her take what she wanted and not just sate his body. She knew Darren would let her do anything she wanted to his body, and it would give him pleasure.

Darren didn't know it, but he was slowly giving her a gift. The gift of finding herself again.

"Condom." She breathed huskily, shoving his boxers off his cock, continuing to alternative between stroking the hard but soft hot flesh and tasting the saltiness of him.

Darren handed her the foil wrapper, and Nessa gave his cock one last lick before she unwrapped the condom and rolled it on Darren's cock. Lifting her gaze, she could see that he was as hungry for her as she was for him.

"How long until the food arrives?"

Darren glanced at his phone. "Bout thirty minutes."

Nessa swung her leg over Darren's legs, lifting her body as she stood his cock up and lowered herself down. The pressure at this angle, as Nessa leaned her head back and rocked against him, one hand on his chest, the other on his leg. The way he was filling her, Nessa needed more of it so she stopped the slow pace and took him all the way into her body.

Darren clasped his hands on her thighs, his bottom lip between his teeth. She paused for a moment, to absorb all the sensations, the tightness, the way the tension in her chest seemed to evaporate. Because it was Darren, and Darren made her feel sexy, and beautiful and safe.

Nessa slowly began to ride Darren, lifting and then sliding back down, the only sounds in the room were their groans, their moans, and the ragged breaths they took. Pleasure shook her body, and when she trembled, Darren lifted himself off the bed, wrapped his arms around her, his hips surging up to meet her thrust for thrust.

The pressure built and built in a delicious wave and when it crashed over her, Darren captured her skin in his mouth as he kissed her, his hands caressing her until his own body jerked, and he came, and Nessa felt every single minute of it.

They kissed a little more, little aftershocks making her clench around Darren's cock that was still buried inside her. Darren kissed her forehead, then her neck and Nessa shuddered.

"Have we got time for a shower?" she asked, and Darren groaned, letting his head rest against hers.

"As much as I would love to shower with you, and we will, I need to feed you and as much as I'd like to brag and say I'm ready to go again, even I need time to recover."

Nessa laughed and slowly rose so that Darren slid out of her, then she strode out of the bedroom and into the shower. The space gave her time to take it all in, and she was surprised that she wasn't panicking. That she hadn't started to count down the minutes or worried that Gavin was out there somewhere.

When she came out of the shower, Darren had left a tee on the side for her, and she wanted to wear his clothes. The tee was sleeveless and came down to her knees. Nessa didn't want to walk around the house in just the tee, so she went and took a clean pair of boxers from Darren's drawer and pulled them on.

Heading downstairs, she lingered in the doorway as Darren put the food on plates, wearing nothing but a pair of grey sweatpants. Nessa had never seen the allure of the hot dudes in grey sweats before but now she got it.

Darren glanced over his shoulder and grinned. "Hey, fresh coffee and food. Eat away. I'm gonna grab a quick shower and then I'll be back."

He kissed her cheek as he slipped by, then rested a hand on her hip. "You look very, very sexy in my clothes."

Nessa was still laughing as she heard Darren jog up the stairs. Sitting down at the kitchen table, Nessa ate her food, and drank her coffee, the smile never leaving her face. Glancing at the clock, she saw that it was around lunchtime. Nessa had slept better than she had in a long-time last night curled up with Darren.

All she had ever wanted in her life was to find someone she felt safe with, someone who would be there for her, to find somewhere she could come home to. She knew it was early days, but Nessa could see herself here, with Darren, and while the prospect of giving herself to someone again terrified her, she knew that Gavin didn't get to steal her happiness.

There was no fucking way she was gonna let him continue to have such a hold on her.

CHAPTER SEVENTEEN

Darren

DARREN WAS STILL GRINNING as he parked his car in his spot beside Rebel Ink. He's fallen hard for Nessa, and after what she told him last night, he didn't want to scare her off, but she seemed content to touch him, to kiss him, to hold his hand as they drove over to Rebel Ink so he could make amends with his family.

Nessa had texted Cliona to ask her if she would meet her for a coffee, and Darren had joked with Nessa to make sure she told all her friends how good he was in bed. She'd smacked him playfully, then froze with fear in her eyes like she was expecting him to react violently. Instead, he's stolen a kiss and the look vanished from her eyes.

"You look very smug." Nessa said as he walked her across the road, the afternoon sun still in the sky.

"I am smug. I had the most beautiful woman in Cork licking my body like her fave lollipop. I have every right to be smug."

Her laughter floated across the wind, as they stopped outside Rebel Books, and Darren cupped her face and kissed her hard on the lips, and when they broke apart, her lips were kiss swollen and sexy.

"I'll come by later after I grovel to Cathal. If that's okay?"

Nessa gave him a devilish smile. "You just want to get me naked again."

"Hell fucking ya, I do. But I was thinking I'd draw you tonight."

He kissed her again, then turned and jogged across the road. When he was on the other side of the road, he called her name, and she looked over at him as he shouted. "Don't forget to tell them how good the sex was!"

Her face went a vivid shade of red as an old woman stopped and looked from Nessa to him and back again, then patted her arm like she was congratulating Nessa. Darren nearly busted a gut laughing as he pushed open the door to Rebel Ink.

"Uncle Darren!"

He crouched down and let Melody wrap her arms around his neck as he hugged her to him, then sat her on the counter so that they were on level. MJ checked his eyes, like she was looking to see if he was still drunk, and that shamed him.

"Hey, I'm sorry for being horrible the other day. I was very sad, and it made me act like an asshole."

MJ didn't say anything, just held out her hand and Darren reached into his pocket and took out a euro, dropping it into the young girl's hand. She put it into the pocket of her hoodie, then looked back at him.

"That's okay. Daddy explained that you were sad. He told me that your mam and dad didn't want you and that Gran was the only parent you had. Like Daddy was to me."

Jesus, that kid was so fucking smart.

"Ya, your dad is right. But I shouldn't have been so mean."

MJ reached out and patted his cheek. "It is sad that your mam and dad acted like they did. It makes me sad to think my mam didn't want me but it's okay. We want you, Uncle Darren. We love you."

Tears prickled his eyes as he just hugged MJ to him. "I love you too, kid."

Darren just stood there, his arms around this amazing fucking kid for a few minutes, then he heard Cathal's voice.

"Hey MJ, your dad is looking for you. Will you give me and Darren a minute?"

MJ turned and gave Cathal a death stare that had his friend's lips twitching like he wanted to laugh.

"Don't be mean. Uncle Darren is sad."

"I promise I won't be mean."

Darren helped MJ down from the counter and she

ducked under the entrance, still glaring at Cathal as she passed. When Cathal checked to make sure that she was out of range, he looked over at Darren with a steely gaze.

"Do you know what it's like to be chewed out by an eight-year-old? Man, that kid is gonna give the world hell when she's older."

Darren's lips curved tugged upward at the corners as he rubbed the back of his neck. "Isaac is a great da." He started then inhaled a breath. "Hoggy, I'm sorry man. I fucking took my grief out on you because after losing Gran, you were the closest thing to family I have. I let my parents get in my head and all the insecurities came flooding out."

Cathal blinked slowly, then slipped his hands into his pockets. "I could have reacted better. I was angry that you weren't coming to me. That somehow, I'd failed ya. And then you said that we all thought you were stupid and an idiot and that's not even remotely true."

Isaac came out from the back and hoisted himself up on the counter. "Cathal's right. When MJ was born, and all the years after, you guys were there with me all the way. Cathal might have been the one to remember all the details I might have forgotten, but Fitz, you made sure that even when things were grave that I laughed. All of it got me through the dark times."

Darren felt embarrassed, and he ribbed the back of his neck as he shrugged. "It wasn't much, really."

"It was man." Isaac said, then he glanced down the hall. "I don't trust just anyone with my girl, Darren. I know that like me, like Cathal, like Shay, you would take a bullet for her and if I thought you were unreliable then I'd not let you spend time with MJ alone."

Darren looked down at his feet, then lifted his gaze back up to look at his family. "I'm still sorry for how I acted. At least let me be man enough to own up to the fact that I made a mistake. I wanna come back to work too."

Cathal smiled. "Apology accepted. And your home, your work, will always be here for ya, Darren. Always."

Darren felt like was gonna bawl again and was glad when Isaac clapped Cathal on the shoulder with a grin. "He's just in a good mood cause Luna is supposed to be back in Cork later for a few days with the band. He's been a grumpy fuck since she went away."

Cathal shoved Isaac and he nearly tumbled off the counter as Cathal gave him the middle finger and they all laughed. And just like that, the world was righted again. Darren was about to ask Cathal about any messages left for him, when the door to Rebel Ink opened.

Oli Scott and his very pregnant partner Niamh Kent came in, the rockstar with a protective arm around his girl's shoulders. There were fist bumps and greetings and then MJ came out and gave Oli and Niamh a hug.

Then she patted Nimah's stomach. "Hello, mini-Scott – it's me MJ."

Niamh grinned at the little girl, as Cathal asked her how the doctors had been.

Oli rolled his eyes. "Nothing. Kid is happy where they are but if there's still no movement by Wednesday, they want to induce."

"I am so ready to be able to tie my own shoes again." Niamh laughed as she rested her hand on her stomach and Darren knew she would be the best ma, and when he told her that, Niamh blushed.

Oli winked at him, then kissed Niamh on the cheek. "Stop trying to charm my missus, Fitz. She only has eyes for me."

"It's okay, Oli." MJ said as she went over to sit down in the waiting area. "Uncle Darren was kissing Nessa a while ago outside the bookshop, so he doesn't want Niamh."

Oli chuckled as Niamh raised her brows and everyone was looking at him. He shrugged and just said. "No comment." Then grinned so wide that there was lots of eye rolling.

Niamh leaned into Oli. "I think I'll leave you boys to talk and head on over to Rebel Books for a while."

When Oli looked like he might argue, Niamh squeezed his arm. "I'm only over the road and maybe MJ could come and hang out with us girls. She can let you know if Mini-Scott decides to make their grand entrance."

MJ immediately jumped up and took Niamh's hand in hers, and even though the rockstar looked like he wanted to wrap his girlfriend and child in bubble wrap, he just kissed her and Niamh and Isaac's little girl left them alone and they all watched to make sure they both arrive in the shop safely.

"Ciara is meeting Charlie at the bookshop for a coffee in a bit. She'll keep an eye on Niamh."

"Jesus, I'm a neurotic fool, aren't I?" Oli murmured, shaking his head.

"Welcome to the terrifying world of being a dad." Isaac said with a snort.

Darren grinned, his eyes looking toward the bookshop for a moment before he joined in with the conversation, and his heart felt a little lighter.

CHAPTER EIGHTEEN

Nessa

THE MOMENT that Nessa walked in the front door of Rebel Books, Cliona had been grinning, obviously having seen her and Darren kissing. Her friend called Molly from the back and asked her to man the shop, then grabbed coffees for them, and they went into the corner of the seating area where Cliona demanded all the filthy details.

Nessa had flushed, and Cliona had howled with laughter, a very smug grin of her own as she said. "I knew that it wouldn't be long before you two got naked."

Rolling her eyes, Nessa told Cliona about what had happened with Darren, then about going to his Gran's and then that she had told him the entire truth about Gavin. And he hadn't looked at her like she was broken or damaged but taken her to bed and made her feel desirable and beautiful.

Cliona opened her mouth to ask another question when the door to Rebel Books opened, and Niamh came in holding Isaac's daughter's hand. They immediately jumped up and fussed over their friend, who growled at them, causing MJ to laugh.

Niamh sent the little girl off to pick out some books, as she lowered herself down onto a chair, then looked Nessa dead in the eye. "What's this I hear about you kissing tattoo artists in the street?"

Nessa lifted her brows, but Niamh just shrugged. "MJ saw you both. Tried to reassure Oli that Darren wasn't flirting with me because he was kissing you."

Nessa thought she would feel a pang of jealously, because Niamh was this gorgeous curvaceous woman that Nessa had always admired. Niamh had been belittled by her ex, a piss poor excuse for a man who had taken Niamh's confidence from her. But Oli, one of the best people Nessa had ever met, had shown Niamh what love truly was and given her everything she had ever wanted.

"I like him," Nessa admitted, leaning her elbows on the table. "I really like him."

"I bet the orgasms helped though, right? I told ya they would."

Niamh barked out a laugh, then winched. "Oh, don't make laugh or I might pee myself."

Sorcha came out from the office and bounded

over, and they chatted for a few minutes until the door opened again and Charlie Coyle came in. The owner of Rebel Racers had been in a few times before, so they called her over to join them.

"I'm meeting Ciara in a bit." She said as she sat down. "Noah and Quinn are having a few days off doing racer shit with Luke before the next race. I came to pick up a book for me for the plane journey."

They all offered her some recommendations, as MJ came over and Sorcha went to help Molly with an issue with the till. Niamh shifted in her seat, told them she needed to walk for a bit. MJ asked her if she should get Oli, but Niamh just smiled.

"No, sweetie, I'm grand, I promise. My back is just a little sore and the walking helps."

Niamh then turned her attention to Charlie. "How are the wedding plans going?"

Charlie rolled her eyes and sighed. "Can I just say that I now appreciate how all our Rebel PR |clients call Andi a ballbuster because she has worked with military precision to put everything in place for the wedding. If left to me and Noah, we'd do a very unromantic courthouse thing and that would be it."

Andi Collins was Charlie's best friend and business partner in Rebel PR. She was also engaged to Declan Walsh, the lead singer of Heartache Melody. If she was as efficient with her management of all the clients as she was with a wedding, then Nessa would believe what Charlie was saying.

"I'm starting to think that Andi will invite us all to some party or gala one day and it will just be here and Dec's wedding. No fuss, just typical Andi. But heaven forbid I might do that with my wedding. She almost fainted when I asked her if we could do it at the race-track where Noah proposed. She told me I could not get married on a racetrack."

"I think that would be a really cool idea," Niamh said, then Nessa watched as pain flashed in her friend's face, and she paled a little.

Sorcha must have noticed as well, because she said she was gonna get Oli, despite Niamh's insistence that she was fine. Nessa helped Niamh walk a little bit as Sorcha decided that she really should get Oli. Nessa had just handed Niamh a class of water. Niamh took a sip, then set the glass down.

"I'm okay. There is no need for all this fuss." Then she grinned mischievously. "Talk to me about Darren. Does he treat you well?"

Nessa nodded her head, leaning against the wall. "He does. I told him everything, Niamh, and it didn't send him running. I think he's one of the good ones."

Niamh's smile widened, as she rested her hands on her bump. "He is. And I should know. I got one myself. Not that it compares to what happened to you, but Brian took away all my confidence and Oli gave it back to me in droves. He didn't run when I pushed him away and even when I almost made the biggest mistake of my life by excluding him from his child's life, he loved me."

Reaching out, Niamh put her hand on Nessa's shoulder. "You deserve someone to love you right, Nessa. Don't be afraid to let him."

Nessa heard raised voices, and Nessa and Niamh walked back around the corner as she watched a man in a mask strike Sorcha across the face when she tried to stop him from coming into the shop. Nessa stepped in front of Niamh, as Sorcha went down to the ground, twisting her leg awkwardly as she fell.

The masked man, and Nessa knew it was a man by the way he stood, the span of his shoulder, slammed the door shut and bolted the latch at the top, then pressed the button to close the blinds and shield them from the outside world. The masked man paced a little, as Sorcha dragged herself out of his way, but then he reached down and grabbed a fistful of her hair, pulled her further into the bookshop.

Cliona moved and lunged for the panic button under the counter by the till. It was then that Nessa remembered that Charlie and little MJ were still in the shop. She was just about to call out a warning when the two of them came down the steps, with Charlie realising what was happening and she made MJ get behind her, the little girl wrapping her arms around the woman.

"The guards are on the way, asshole. Get the fuck out!" Sorcha said from the floor, and Nessa almost thew up when the man kicked Sorcha in the stomach, and the woman did throw up.

The masked man went back to pacing, and Nessa's heart was beating so fast as Cliona went over to where Sorcha was breathing hard. Nessa felt frozen to the spot. Memories of what had happened to her came rushing back as she starred at Sorcha, heard the wheeze that came from bruised or broken ribs.

"I want my dad." MJ whimpered from behind Charlie, and Nessa snapped out of her panic. There was more than her to worry about and they all needed to get the man out of the shop before he hurt anyone else.

Hopefully, Molly was locked in the office and was on the phone to the guards.

"There's money in the till, if that's what your after." Nessa said, a slight tremble in her voice. "You can take it and go. You don't have to hurt anyone else."

Laughter, familiar and terrifying, punched Nessa in the gut and she grabbed Niamh's hand as she let out a shocked. "No."

The masked man ripped off his mask and tossed it on the ground, and Nessa's worst nightmare come to life. A sneer twisted lips that had taunted her, and lips that had kissed her. pinpoint pupils told Nessa that the man who has almost killed her two years ago was off his face, the jerky movement told her that he had come to do what he had said when he told her he would kill her.

Demented eyes watched Nessa as he smiled. It was a cruel and vicious smile that chilled Nessa's blood and made her want to cower from him. He saw her flinch, and it pleased him that he could still scare her like that.

"Gavin, let these people go. It's me you want."

Gavin tilted his head slightly, clearly amused as he gestured with his hands. "Why would I do that, Nessa. These people are responsible for taking you from me. For making you think you could live without me. They must be punished too."

It was then that Gavin took the gun out of the waistband of his jeans and pointed it right at Nessa.

CHAPTER NINETEEN

Nessa

THERE'S a moment of stunned silence when Gavin brandished the gun, the only sound Nessa could hear was the beat of her own heart in her ears. He's holding the gun the same way they do the gangster films that he liked to watch, tilted sideways but pointed directly at Nessa.

If he fired at her now, then there was every chance that a bullet would hurt Niamh and the baby. That MJ could get shot. Her panic threatened to undo her, but Nessa told herself that she had to hold it together, that she could not break down and let him win, and that she needed to keep him occupied for as long as possible to try and make sure her friends were safe.

A siren sounded in the distance and anger flashed

in Gavin's eyes. "Get down on the fucking ground. Get the fuck down."

Cliona and Sorcha were already on the ground, and Charlie pulled MJ over by the counter, putting MJ behind her, leaving just Nessa and Niamh standing. Gavin took a step forward and shook the gun.

"I said get down on the fucking ground bitch. You should be used to being on your fucking knees."

Nessa would have been embarrassed if not for the terror in her spine. Instead, she steeled herself and looked Gavin dead in the eyes.

"You cannot expect a pregnant woman to get down on the ground, Gavin. Let me get her a chair."

Gavin sneered, shaking the gun again. "The bitch either gets down on the fucking ground, Nessa or I will kick the fucking baby from her stomach. You remember how hard I can kick, dontcha. Blondie sure does."

Sorcha spat at his feet. "Go fuck yourself, asshole."

Nessa wanted to keep Gavin's focus on her. She reluctantly stepped away from Niamh, dragged a chair from the café area, and then gave Gavin her back as she helped Niamh sit down in the chair. Her friend clutched her stomach to protect her child, but Nessa just stepped in front of Niamh.

The sirens grew louder, and Gavin let loose a slew of curses, then reached into the pocket of his jacket, and took out a bag of white powder. Cocaine. Nessa just stood there as he emptied some powder onto his hand, lifted his hand to his nose, snorted it loudly, and then wiped his nose.

The disgust on Nessa's face must have shown because Gavin sneered. "You don't get to judge me, bitch. You ruined my life! You made me this way, seducing me, and then you made sure that I couldn't enjoy my life by having me on curfew. I was content, Nessa, really fucking content to know that you were this lamb, hiding away during the day, terrified of me."

Niamh touched the back of her leg, letting her know that she wasn't alone, comforting her even though she must be petrified.

"I could have been content with that, knowing you were fucking suffering as much as me." Gavin tapped the gun at the side of his head. "I could see it in my head, the way you looked when you felt that I had come to deliver your death. It was that look in your eyes that I imagined in my head as I stroked myself."

Bile threatened to claw its way up her throat. He was even more sick than Nessa thought.

"And then I saw you, with *him*." Gavin continued, tapping the gun against his forehead and Nessa had the insane wish that he would prove himself the moron he was and do the world a favour by blowing what little brains he had out.

"I followed you to his house. I knew you were fucking him. I could *feel* it. In here." He said as he tapped the cup on his chest. Then you kissed him, for everyone to see. You belong to me! You are mine and you don't get to disrespect me by whoring around on me."

"I don't belong to you, Gavin," Nessa said softly, but defiantly.

"YOU GODDAM FUCKING DO!" He screamed and Nessa flinched, her knees trembling, but Niamh kept her hand firmly on her leg.

Gavin prepped another bump, and snorted, his eyes still on them. Nessa saw the blood trickling down his nose before he wiped it away. "I should have walked right into that tattoo shop and put a bullet in his head for daring to touch what's mine. He put his hands on you, Nessa. He doesn't get to live after that."

There was lead in her stomach, as she put her hand to her throat. "Gavin, he hasn't done anything wrong. It's all me. I told them terrible things about you. Embellished the truth. Let them go and then I'm all yours. We can talk."

Gavin's eyes flared as he came over and wrapped his free hand around her throat squeezing until Nessa had to concentrate to breathe and she could smell the rancid stench of his breath. She heard shouts that were quickly quietened when Gavin pointed the gun at Niamh.

Nessa reacted before she had a moment to think, remembered what the guard who had rescued her told her, to always go for the nose, throat, or balls of any man who tried to hurt her. bringing her knee up hard, Gavin let loose a yowl and staggered back.

"Score one for Miss Congeniality bitches!" Sorcha cheered. but her cheer was short-lived as Gavin roared and lashed out with his hand, striking Nessa across the face and she went down to the ground. It was only when her face throbbed and she felt wetness on her cheek, did she realize that Gavin had hit her with the gun.

Nessa looked down at the blood on her hand, and she was back in that apartment, looking up at Gavin with death in his eyes.

"You belong to me, Nessa! Me. You'll never escape me. I own you bitch."

Hands in her hair, her body screamed in pain, as Nessa tried to blink the blood from her eyes. Her leg banged off the door, off the wall as Gavin dragged her toward the bathroom, continuing his rant that she was his, that without him she was worthless, unloved, unwanted. Nessa believed him, even as he dragged her body up, and she looked at the water in the tub.

"I'm gonna kill you. I'm gonna hold you as the life goes out and you will die, knowing that you will always be mine and mine alone. Fucking bitch, drugging me. ungrateful whore!"

Gavin lifted her broken body and shoved her head under the water, a death grip on her hair as water filled her lungs and she jerked in his grasp. She didn't want to die. She didn't want to die.

Nessa blinked out of the memory when Gavin grabbed her by the hair, yanked her to her feet, and then kissed her hard on the mouth. Her gorge rose and she shoved at his chest until he released her.

"Now, when you die, the last taste you'll have is of my lips. I'll tell him that when I walk out of here. That I tasted you again. Maybe I should fuck you here and now, with all the witnesses. They'll tell your tattoo prick that you cried out in pleasure because you're a whore who should be on your knees thanking me for paying you any attention!"

Nessa glanced behind her, relieved to see that Niamh had given MJ headphones, the little girl keeping her eyes closed as Charlie kept a protective arm around her. All Nessa wanted in this moment was to get all the people she cared about out of the shop. Her life didn't really matter once they were all safe.

But her life mattered to these women. To her friends, her found family. Her life mattered to Darren, who had just lost his Gran and might lose Nessa even before they had gotten a chance to give things a go.

Lights flashed outside, and Gavin turned away from her to go to the window and look out through the blinds. He cursed and slumped down on one of the chairs. Nessa turned to check on Niamh, and then over at Cliona and Sorcha, whose leg was twisted in a way that reminded Nessa of her own broken leg after Gavin had beaten her.

Gavin wanted her dead, of that Nessa was certain. But who else was he willing to take with her as collateral damage? Nessa wasn't about to let that happen.

Gavin didn't get to win today. He didn't get to be the one holding all the power.

The phone rang on the counter, and Gavin jerked to his feet. The phone rang and rang until Gavin came over and ripped the phone from its socket and flung it across the room with a scream that was full of rage, full of venom.

"That was probably the guards wanting to talk to you." Nessa broached, and Gavin spun in her direction.

"I don't care who da fuck it was. I don't want to talk to anyone!"

"Then what exactly do you want, Gavin? What's the plan here?"

CHAPTER TWENTY

Darren

THEY HAD NO MORE clients for the day, so Cathal had swung the closed sign on the door and they had all just chatted for a while. Oli joked that Jameson was trying to make sure that he got home from the mini showcase before the baby arrived because Danika kept teasing him that she was gonna be the first one to hold the baby beside the parents.

They had been chatting for a while when Darren heard the sound of sirens, of slammed doors, and shouts. Oli turned round, and they watched as barricades were set up around Rebel Books, and Garda closed off the street.

"What the fuck?" Oli said as he yanked open the door and rushed out into the street, with everyone else rushing out behind him.

Armed response vehicles pulled up as they reached the cordon, and a guard pushed Oli back. "Sir, ya need to take a step back."

"People we love are in there. My ... my pregnant girlfriend, his little girl and our friends are in there. What the fuck happened?"

"I can't discuss an active incident, sir. Please step back and stay out of the way."

Darren glanced over his shoulder to see Cathal holding Isaac back, and his face was distraught. Darren's heart sank even as the worry for Nessa flooded through him. Oli was still arguing with the guard at the barrier when someone called Isaac's name.

A man who looked familiar jogged up to the barrier and spoke to the guard that had been hassling Oli, before he jumped the barrier and walked over to them.

"James, MJ is in there. MJ and Ciara." Issac said, and the guard looked shocked. "What's going on?"

"Isaac! Isaac!" Isaac whirled round at the sound of Ciara's voice as she pushed through the crowd, and suddenly his girlfriend Ciara was in his arms, they were hugging. "Oh thank god, I thought you were in there, you and MJ."

Ciara looked toward the bookshop, and her eyes widened. "Oh no. Is she okay, are they okay?"

Darren wanted to know that too and they all turned to look at this guard James.

He offered them a grim smile, then introduced

himself. "I'm Declan's brother, James. Sorry to be meeting most of you like this. Okay, so what do we know? An armed assailant entered the premises and locked the doors. We think that it's all staff and no customers, but we can't confirm that until we can get the lay of the land. A panic button was pushed inside the bookshop just before a call was made by a staff member who was hiding in the office. She identified herself as Molly."

Shit, that meant that everyone else was being held hostage by the madman.

"Molly told us that she saw the attacker hurt Sorcha Healy before she locked herself in the office."

Ciara gasped, and Issac hugged her tight. "Sorcha's her cousin."

"Molly managed to tell us that Sorcha was alive before her phone died." James glanced around. "We think the man holding them hostage is Gavin Philips, Nessa Kennedy's ex-boyfriend. I was one of the arresting officers who was first on the scene and I've kept an eye on Nessa over the last two years."

"You're the guard who stayed with her in the hospital so she wasn't alone when she woke up?"

James shifted his gaze to Darren. "Nessa told you about me?"

"Yeah, she did. How the hell did this, Gavin get this close to her?" Darren asked, hating the fact that they were all trapped inside with this madman.

"The conditions of his curfew state that he can be

out during daylight hours. He has a tag and from that, we know that he is in there. I promise you all that we are doing all we can to get your people out. I'll keep you all updated as soon as I know more."

James looked over at Oli. "The pregnant woman is Niamh, right?"

"My whole fucking world is in that shop." Oli sounded like he was tortured and maybe he was.

James just nodded his head, jumped back over the barrier, and went over to a tall Asian-looking guard, who glanced back at them all after a few minutes. Darren had never felt more useless in all his life. Then it hit him.

"Oli, didn't you get a whole new security system set up in the shop? Would your team not be able to get eyes inside?"

Oli's eyes widened, and he pulled out his phone. "Darren, I could kiss ya mate."

Walking away from the group, Oli spoke down the phone and asked some fella named Gus if he had eyes inside the shop. Then his voice rose. "Gus, I don't fucking care if it's not something that I should be seeing. The guards need eyes inside the shop and we've got it. Send me the link, please. Can you tell if everyone is okay?"

Oli nodded his head, then thanked the man as he ended the call. His phone pinged and Isaac came over and glanced over Oli's shoulder, as did Darren. He saw Nessa standing in front of Niamh, who was sitting down. He saw Cliona, and he saw a beat-up Sorcha looking like she'd gone a few rounds with his cousin Eve. His eyes widened when he saw Charlie Coyle sitting down by the counter's corner.

Darren's heart sank when he couldn't see MJ and Isaac let loose a strangled sound

"Where's MJ? Where the fuck is she? Why can't I see her?" Issac rambled, and Darren knew his friend would not be content until his little girl was in his arms, safe and sound.

Oli stared at the screen, then let loose a sigh of relief. "Charlie is blocking her. I can see MJ's hand in Charlie's. She's okay, Isaac, she's okay. Charlie's got her."

Isaac swayed on his feet, Cathal steadying him until Ciara wrapped her arms around his waist. Oli whistled, and James looked in his direction before jogging over. Oli handed him his phone, and James looked at it. "Fuck, can someone call Andi and tell her Charlie is in the shop. She'll contact Noah before it gets on the news."

"I've got Andi. But I'll need my phone back." Oli said, as James sent the link to his own phone, then told them not to watch it, drive themselves insane.

Oli called Andi, and Cathal said he would ring Jameson. Having called Andi, Oli swore and said he needed to call Danika. As if she had been conjured, the woman ran through the crowd and looked at Oli, who just nodded.

"Why the fuck are you numpties not going in there!" Danika yelled, shaking her head. "Standing 'round doing nothing. Useless pricks."

Oli pulled her in for a hug. "Shut up, Dani. Just shut up."

Under normal circumstances, that would have made Darren laugh, but this was not the time to be laughing at stupid shit. Oli's phone rang, and he looked at it, took a deep breath, and then answered.

"Noah, she's alive. She's alive and she is right at this moment, shielding Isaac's MJ from a man with a gun. I'm not sending you the link when you are halfway across the world so don't ask me to." Oli nodded at whatever Noah was saying down the phone, obviously in bits that his fiancé was in danger when he wasn't even in the country.

"Declan's brother is on the scene, and he's keeping us updated. I swear to you that I will keep you updated. Our girls are strong. They are fucking warriors."

Oli and Noah hung up, and they all stood around and waited and waited but still there was nothing. Despite the fact that Oli had promised not to watch the video, he couldn't help himself and Darren looked over his shoulder.

Darren saw Gavin shouting at Nessa, then snort what Darren assumed was cocaine before he lifted his head and looked back at Nessa. There was blood dripping down his nose, his mouth moving but they couldn't hear anything.

"I wish we could get fucking sound. Why the fuck didn't I get the place wired for sound." Oli mumbled to himself; his eyes glued to the screen.

Nessa said something to Gavin, and he stalked over and wrapped a hand around Nessa's throat and Darren let loose a strangled sound. Everyone got riled up and then Gavin pointed his gun right at Niamh. Oli cried out and grabbed Darren's arm, both of them unable to look away.

Darren watched as Nessa kneed Gavin in the balls. He stumbled backward, but then he lashed out, striking Nessa across the face and she crumbled to the ground. Darren swore, as Nessa looked up at Gavin, this vacant look in her eyes like she wasn't there. Gavin yanked Nessa up by her hair, then kissed her hard on the mouth. Darren had to walk away because he couldn't watch whatever Gavin had planned for Nessa. Oli told them that Gavin had just ripped out the phone, before tossing it across the room.

CHAPTER TWENTY-ONE

Nessa

"WHAT DO I WANT? What do I fucking want?"

Gavin paced again, scratching his head with the muzzle of the gun. He looked outside again, then turned back to her. "I want you gone. I want you dead. I want to go back to before I laid eyes on you at the goddamn party, and you begged me to make you mine with those come fuck me eyes."

Nessa folded her arms across her chest. "I was fifteen, Gavin. I was a child. You were an adult. I don't deny that I wanted to sleep with you then, but you wanted it as much as I did."

"You kept saying that. They kept saying that in court. Make me sound like a filthy pedo."

"If the shoe fits, scumbag," Sorcha muttered, and Cliona clamped a hand over her mouth to stop their friend from letting her mouth get her into any more trouble.

Gavin snarled, pointing the gun in Sorcha's direction. "Keep running you're mouth blondie and I'll put something in your mouth that will shut you up."

Sorcha snorted and smacked Cliona's hand away. "Bitch please, I've sucked on ice lollies with more girth than you've got."

Gavin slid his gaze to where MJ was. "Maybe I should break her in."

"You do that and there will be a queue of people wanting to cut off your limp dick. I'll be first in the fucking line. Fucking coward."

Jesus, Sorcha was gonna get herself killed.

Gavin's face went a vicious shade of red. He stalked over and grabbed Sorcha by her hurt leg and yanked her across the floor. Cliona grabbed for her, but Gavin pointed the gun at her. Sorcha lunged forward and sank her teeth into his leg or at least tried to. Gavin yelped, then coldcocked Sorcha across the head. Blood seeped into her blonde hair, as she slumped down, eyes shut, but Nessa was relieved to see that Sorcha's chest was rising and falling.

Gavin looked down at Sorcha, then back at Nessa. "You used to be like her, remember? A mouthy little bitch who needed a man like me to break her in. Did I tell you your friend confronted me? Maggie? That fat bitch got in my face and told me that what I was doing was wrong and that you'd see it soon enough. I had someone rough her up. She stopped bitching after that."

Nessa shivered at the cold in her bones. She didn't know what to do. She didn't know what to say to try and find a way that this ended without any more violence. He'd see through her lies if she tried to coax him upstairs to the apartment so she could trick him and lock them both inside. She would be trapped with him but at least the others would be safe.

"My dad cut me out of the business after court. Oh, he kept me on to do the dirty jobs. But I was no longer working with him. He told me his counterparts didn't want to work with someone who was convicted of beating a woman. Fucking criminals with morals. And then someone told them you were fifteen and deals started going away."

Gavin tapped the side of his head. He was starting to look tired, though another bump of coke would get him all riled up again. "I can't go to prison. We both die here."

"Your dad will get you out of it, Gavin. He always does."

Gavin shook his head. "Not this time. Too public. Too fucking public. You don't think I know who the pregnant bitch is dating, who her brother is? Or who the dyke bitch is dating? This story doesn't just make the six o'clock news. It's international."

Nessa stepped forward, holding her hands up. "Then let the rockstar's pregnant girlfriend go. Let the child go, Gavin. Let everyone else walk out that door and you and me can finish this. It started with us. It needs to finish with us."

Gavin tapped the gun against his forehead three times. "I need to think."

Cliona crouched holding her hands up as Gavin's gaze darted to her. "Can I at least get Niamh a drink? The last thing you need is her or the baby being hurt."

Gavin nodded his head as he sat down on the stairs and buried his face in his hands. Nessa turned and gave Niamh's shoulder a squeeze as Nessa heard Charlie ask MJ if she was okay.

The little girl had taken out her earphones and nodded, then looked at her and Charlie. "I'm okay, but I think Niamh might have wet herself."

Everyone turned to look at Niamh and at the wetness on her leggings. There was a pool of water by her feet and the woman had a tear coming down her face. Nessa crouched down and took Niamh's hands in hers.

"Niamh, did your waters break?"

More tears slipped from her eyes as she nodded, then flashed Nessa a weak smile. "Looks like Mini-Scott likes to make a spectacular entrance just like their dad."

This was bad. This was really bad.

"Are you having contractions?" Charlie asked softly and Niamh nodded.

"Started when he took out the gun. I'm trying not

to freak out because I don't want to freak out MJ, but I'm scared. I can't have my baby here. I need Oli."

Nessa spun round and got to her feet. "You need to let her go. There is a baby on the way and she needs a hospital. For fuck sake, Gavin. If anything happens to her or the baby, your father will put a bullet in your head himself, if Oli doesn't kill you himself. I'll help him."

"Me too..." groaned Sorcha as she put her hand to her head, and it came away bloody.

Charlie had stripped off her hoody, and put it down on the ground as she helped Niamh to lie down. MJ took Niamh's hand and started to sing softly. Charlie then grabbed Cliona's jumper that the woman held out to her and placed it under Niamh's head.

Niamh let loose a moan, her hand going to her stomach. Nessa waited and watched until the pain seemed to pass, and Niamh closed her eyes. MJ kept on singing as Gavin took in the scene.

He pointed the gun at Nessa. "This is all your fault!"

Nessa shook her head, not willing to shoulder all of the blame. "I'm not the one who took a group of women hostage and refuses to let a woman in labour and a small girl go free. You are the one holding the gun, Gavin. Everything that happens from now on, that's all up to you."

Cliona stepped up beside Nessa. "Can I go to the office to get some dry clothes for Niamh, please? If you're not gonna let her go, we need to make her as comfortable as possible. It can't be nice to be sitting in all her wet clothes."

Gavin waved the gun. "No fucking funny business or I swear I'll start shooting."

Cliona shook her head. "That's the last thing I want. I promise you that."

As Cliona went to get some dry clothing, Nessa watched Gavin take out his phone, and then he pressed something, and they all heard a voice saying clearly.

"According to multiple sources, there is a hostage situation at a bookstore in Cork City. The bookstore is owned by Niamh Kent, sister of rockstar Jameson Kent and partner of Oli Scott. Believed to be in the bookshop is also the girlfriend of Danika Keane, other staff of the bookstore, and a young child who was with the pregnant Ms. Kent at the time of the incident. All attempts to contact the perpetrator have failed. Stay tuned for more updates. Zara King, Virgin Media News."

Gavin got up and kicked a chair halfway across the room.

Sorcha dragged herself over toward them, glancing at Gavin before she turned and rolled her eyes. "Other staff? Not even a notable mention. That hurts more than any bitch slap from coke head over there."

Nessa couldn't help it, couldn't stop the giggle that escaped her lips, she clamped a hand over her mouth to stop any more laughter from slipping out even as

Sorcha grinned, showing off her bloody teeth as she leaned against the counter.

Cliona came back out with the clean clothing, and they blocked Gavin's view as Cliona stripped off Niamh's wet clothes and put a blanket over her legs. Nessa can tell that the poor woman is trying not to freak out, but Nessa is a little freaked out herself.

Locking over to where Gavin sat on the steps, Nessa could see that the anger had drained from his eyes and had been replaced with an expression of hopelessness. That was more dangerous than his anger, because when you lost hope, you were capable of anything.

Nessa knew that time was running out and she needed to find a way to get the gun away from Gavin. Even if it meant she had to be the one to put a bullet in him.

Chapter Twenty-Two

Nessa

NOTHING HAPPENS for the longest time. Gavin remained on the steps, obsessively checking his phone for news updates. Niamh's contractions were still a long time apart, and Nessa knew that gave them some time before things got even more serious than they already were. Her friend had been uncomfortable lying down so they had propped her up against the counter.

MJ had stopped singing, and Charlie had gone back to shielding MJ in case Gavin decided to start shooting. Nessa had cleaned up the floor a little, moved the wet chair Niamh had been sitting on, and replaced it with a dry one. Then she had taken a seat and looked around at her friends.

Cliona had Sorcha next to her, the blonde woman resting her head on Cliona's shoulder. Nessa could tell that she was in pain, but there was this fearless expression on her face that Nessa both admired and was terrified by. Gavin had already singled out Sorcha because he despised a strong woman, and was intimidated by them. He relished in breaking them, like he had broken her.

Or tried to...she was still here fighting.

"I need to go to the bathroom."

Nessa glanced over at the little girl, her heart sinking as she looked back at Gavin. He wasn't paying attention to any of them. Her eyes meet Cliona's, who nodded, slowly getting to her feet with her hands held out in submission.

Gavin jerked his head up, and the gun in Cliona's direction. "Sit the fuck back down."

"Okay, I will. But can I please take MJ to the bathroom? She's just a little girl. I don't want this to be any more traumatic for her. The bathroom is just there in between the two offices. You can walk over with us and wait while she goes. Please."

Cliona was being as compliant as she possible could, more polite than Nessa might have been. Gavin liked that. He gave a sharp nod of his head, then got up off the steps as Cliona slowly walked over to where Charlie had MJ shielded, took her hand and without looking at Gavin, took MJ into the bathroom, closed the door but didn't lock it.

Gavin took out his phone again, pressed play on the video and the female reporters voice said. "That's correct. New reports from the scene that entrepreneur and CEO of the Formula 1 team Rebel Racers, Charlotte Coyle is also a hostage in the bookshop. Charlotte is the fiancée of Noah Donovan who Virgin Media has learned is currently in Denmark."

Gavin's gaze snapped in Charlie's direction, and she tensed.

"Zara, have the gardaí revealed any motive for the incident?"

"No, in fact they have been keeping all media as far away from the scene as possible. They also have the added pressure that several of the partners and family members of those inside the bookshop are on the scene. The gardaí are having to hold them back to prevent them from trying to gain entry to the premises."

The news went back to talking about other notable events, and Gavin shoved his phone back into his pocket as Cliona and MJ came out of the bathroom. MJ went straight back to Charlie and cuddled up to her side. Charlie stroked the little girl's hair and MJ closed her eyes.

Nessa hoped she could get a little rest, but knew it was probably impossible. Gavin started to head back toward the steps, then turned to look to where Charlie sat beside Niamh and MJ.

"You own Rebel Racers."

Charlie lifted her chin. "Ya, I do."

"Then you've got money, right? You've probably got a private plane."

Charlie swallowed hard, kept on stroking MJ's hair. "I've got money. I can get you some but the kinda money you will need, that's not a quick trip to an ATM. And the private plane is currently in Denmark with my fiancé and his teammates. Though I suspect it will arrive back at Cork Airport sooner than planned."

Gavin snarled in frustration, then went back over to the steps and sat down again, putting his head in his hands with the gun hanging from his grasp. Nessa's heart raced as she considered rushing Gavin to see if she could knock the gun from his hand.

But this wasn't the movies, and she wasn't Jennifer Lopez fighting back against her abuser.

Niamh let loose a moan of pain, sweat beading on her forehead as Charlie gripped her hand, and told her everything would be okay, which made Niamh laugh.

"I'm not so sure about that," Niamh said through gritted teeth. "I'm in labour while being held hostage by a man waving a gun about. The father of my child is apparently being held back by the guards. I had it all planned ya know? My bag's been packed for weeks. I have my birthing playlist. I said I'd not have an epidural so that I could feel everything, but can I just say that any fucking drugs would be good right now."

"I know I'm a poor substitute for Oli, but I'm here for you." Charlie said in response, as Niamh shifted slightly, then swore, before she closed her eyes. Nessa might have thought she was sleeping, but Niamh then blinked open her eyes.

"How did you meet Oli?"

Charlie grinned, lifted her gaze to Gavin before dropping her gaze once more. "Andi. We had just set up Rebel PR and we went to this big industry party in Manchester. She had a list of stars that she wanted to manage. She made a beeline for Oli and JJ, told them that they would regret it if they didn't get signed by her, because she would make them a hell of a lot of money and that we were worth the investment."

"Oh my god, that so sounds like Andi. What did Oli say?"

Charlie pressed her lips together. "I can't."

"Oh, well now you have to tell me," Niamh demanded, and Charlie chuckled.

"He told her that he loved a woman who took charge and he'd happily let her order him about during sex."

Niamh's already flushed cheeks darkened. "No!"

"Yup," Charlie told Niamh. "But Andi turned round and told him that he could get that idea out of his dirty little mind because she didn't fuck her clients and Oli was gonna be her client before the night was out. Twenty minutes later, Andi had signed contracts from Oli and JJ."

"Does Declan know that Oli tried to get Andi into bed?" Niamh asked, and Charlie nodded.

"Ya, but Oli only did it to see if Andi was the real

deal. If she had jumped into bed with him, then Oli would have told her to fuck right off. From what I hear, you had him lusting after you for months before you succumbed to his charms."

Niamh smiled softly but didn't say anything else about it. Instead, she said to Charlie. "I never thought I could love anyone as much as I love Oli. How much I already love our baby."

Charlie offered Niamh a smile. "I understand. I loved Noah when we were kids, and never stopped loving him even when we were apart. We've been through the ringer a few times."

"It makes you stronger."

"I'm not sure about that," Charlie said as she glanced around, then let loose a sigh. "I'm pregnant."

Niamh's eyes widened and she opened her mouth to speak, however Charlie shook her head. "The doctor confirmed it today. I've felt off for a while, but I thought it was wedding stress."

"Noah's gonna be over the moon."

Charlie shook her head. "I can't tell him. It's too early. I can't put that on him when he is so close to achieving his dreams. Last year, Noah had some mental health issues. We got him help but we almost ended things because of it. We tried for a baby, and I got pregnant. We made plans and then I miscarried. We tried again, I miscarried again."

"Oh Charlie." Niamh had tears in her eyes as she gave Charlie's hand a squeeze.

"The doctor told us to wait a while before trying again. Noah fell into a slump after the second miscarriage, and he had that crash in qualifying. In his whole career, Noah has never crashed a car. So, we decided to wait. And now, I'm pregnant again. I can't tell him. Not until the final race of the season is over. I can't be the reason why Noah is off his game, and he's not crowned World Champion."

"Noah wouldn't want you to go through this alone." Niamh said as she shifted again.

"I know. But I have Andi and Ciara. I'll be alright."

"And us. You've got us now too." Sorcha said from where she dozed.

Niamh shifted again, and Nessa paid close attention as Niamh said. "Not to panic anyone, even though I'm panicking enough for all of us, but I really, really have the urge to start pushing. Oh dear god, that fucking hurts."

CHAPTER TWENTY-THREE

Darren

DARREN HAD NEVER BEEN good at just waiting around. He was bouncing out of his skin waiting for the guards to do anything to try and put an end to this ordeal. But all they seemed to do was mill about and assess the scene.

Complete fucking bullshit.

He was worried about Nessa; however, his worry didn't compare to Oli and Issac. Both men had been pacing for a solid thirty minutes now, and Ciara had been left in charge of watching the video feed since neither man could bear to watch it.

Darren heard Ciara gasp then she sucked in a breath as both Isaac and Oli came running back over, but Ciara shielded the video from view as she held Oli's gaze. Darren was struck by just how freaked out

Ciara had been when she first started dating Isaac and was around all these famous people. But now, she calmly reached out and took Oli's hand.

"It looks like Niamh has gone into labour. Her waters have just broken."

The devastation on Oli's face was heartbreaking.

"Let me see. Gimmie the phone."

Ciara handed the phone to Oli, and he glanced at the screen. "And here I thought our biggest worry would be paparazzi trying to sneak in to take photos. Fuck she looks so scared."

Darren glanced over Oli's shoulder, saw Cliona get to her feet and point to the bathroom. Then as Gavin jerked his head, Cliona took MJ to the bathroom. Gavin took out his phone and looked pissed off as he watched something on it.

Danika, who had been sitting across the road on the footpath outside Rebel Ink, let loose a shout, then held up her phone. "It's Cliona!"

She came running over as she said down the phone. "Cliona! Cliona!"

"Okay MJ," came Cliona's voice on the other end. "I'm gonna hide my phone in your pocket. I have it so that they can hear us, but we can't hear them, so Gavin won't know you have my phone. But I can hold it if you're too scared."

"It's okay, I can be brave. My daddy's gonna be very worried."

"He is. But hopefully he is listening in now. We won't let Gavin hurt you MJ."

They heard the flush of a toilet, then footsteps as they walked outside. They watched on the video as MJ went straight back to Charlie, who hugged the little girl to her, and Charlie stroked the little girl's hair and MJ closed her eyes.

The madman turned his eyes toward Charlie and MJ, and for a horrible moment, Darren feared that somehow, he knew that MJ had a phone on her. "You own Rebel Racers."

Charlie lifted her chin. "Ya, I do."

"Then you've got money, right? You've probably got a private plane."

They listened as Charlie told Gavin that she had money, that it wouldn't be easy to get that kinda money for him, and that her private plane was currently in another country. Gavin sounded pissed off when he went back to the steps and sat down again, his head in his hands with the gun hanging from his grasp.

A moan of pain sounded, and they heard Charlie tell Niamh that everything would be okay. Oli's shoulders sagged as he heard Niamh laugh, then she said. "I'm not so sure about that. I'm in labour while being held hostage by a man waving a gun about. The father of my child is probably being held back by the guards. I had it all planned ya know? My bag's been packed for weeks. I have my birthing playlist. I said I'd not have an epidural so that I could feel everything, but can I just say that any fucking drugs would be good right now."

They listened as Charlie told Niamh how she and Andi had met Oli and JJ, and that brought a smile to Oli's lips, though it quickly fell. They listened as Isaac shouted James's name, the guard striding over just as they heard Charlie say. "I'm pregnant."

Oli put the phone off the loudspeaker and looked at everyone around him. "No one speaks a word of this to Noah. He doesn't deserve to learn he's gonna be a dad while the woman he loves has a gun pointed at her."

Switching back on the loudspeaker, Darren knew that when they heard the next part of Charlie's story, that not a single one of them would utter a word to Noah. From the look on Ciara's face, she already knew all about Charlie's miscarriages, and then Charlie confirmed it.

"I know. But I have Andi and Ciara. I'll be alright."

"And us. You've got us now too," they heard Sorcha mumble, and Ciara put her hand to her throat.

They watched as Niamh shifted again, and even as she spoke, telling them not to panic, Niamh was pale, and her expression was one of sheer terror. "Not to panic anyone, even though I'm panicking enough for all of us, but I really, really have the urge to start push-ing. Oh, dear god, that fucking hurts."

"Fucking hell, I need to get in there. I need to be with her." Oli said, a tear trickling down his face.

Danika wrapped her arms around him as James took Danika's phone and handed it off to his partner.

"She'll be okay, Oli. They both will. They all will."

Darren hoped that was true for everyone. Oli's eyes were trained on the front of Rebel Books, his eyes moving rapidly as he wet his lips. "There's a way in through the back. A door that leads into a service entrance and it opens in the basement of the bookshop. It's never used but when we had the security company install the new measures, I made sure that they hooked that door up as well. Why the fuck didn't I think of it before."

James reached out and squeezed Oli's shoulder. "I'll let armed response know. That might just get us in the door."

It would take armed response time to formulate a plan. They would need to get the building's blueprints, then find out if the security has been switched off on the door, or at least that's what Darren assumed anyways from all the action movies he'd watched.

They needed to get someone inside the building to help and even though he had fallen in love with Nessa, he was the one that was the least emotional about it all.

Fuck...he was in love with Nessa.

Oli put in a call to his security company as Andi Collins pushed through the crowd, her face tearstained as she strode up to her future brother-in-law, and demanded to be told why they were dragging their heels and not going in to get their people out.

Darren glanced over his shoulder toward the book-shop, and felt eyes on him, tuning back to see Cathal watching him like he knew exactly what Darren was thinking of doing. His friend shook his head, but Darren had already made his mind up.

What he needed was a distraction. To be fair, it was him that usually volunteered to be the distraction. Not that this situation called for him getting almost naked and drawing a crowd to him. No, he needed people to ignore him so he could slip away.

"Darren, don't."

He gave Cathal a shrug of his shoulders, then gave Isaac a little shove. His friend stumbled back and let loose a curse. Everyone turned to look at Isaac and Darren bolted, pushing his way through the crowd, and hopping over the cordon with ease. He heard people shout his name, and heard the guards telling him to stop but Darren kept moving.

He darted down one of the laneways and came out behind the row of businesses. He spotted the stairs that led down to the basement level, and he just fucking hoped and prayed that when he opened the door, there would be no alarm on it. Shit, he should have really asked about that before he ran off but now it was too late to go back and get the information.

Footsteps sounded over his shoulder and Darren glanced behind him to see the guard James running toward him. Darren went down the steps, and crouched in the corner, and James followed suit. The guard looked at him with a grim expression and when he might have spoken, Darren cut right across him.

"I'm going in there. You're gonna have to shoot me if you want me not to."

James rolled his eyes, shifting so that he looked into the small window in the basement. "Thought you might need some backup. And the code to unlock the door might come in handy too."

"Sarcastic much?" Darren asked him with a snort.

James grinned, taking popping a button on his shirt. "When you're the middle triplet you learn to stand out in any way you have to. Now, let's stop talking about my sparkling wit and figure out a plan of action."

CHAPTER TWENTY-FOUR

Nessa

NIAMH WAS NOT in a good way.

Gavin took one look at her as Niamh screamed at a contraction and looked like he wanted to vomit. Nessa knew that someone was gonna have to check and see how far Niamh was dilated, though none of them was prepared for what Sorcha said.

"Cliona, you should be the one to check. You've the most experience with sticking your fingers into vagina."

Charlie barked out a laugh, and Nessa shook her head as Cliona glared at the blonde woman, who just shrugged. "What? It's the truth."

Niamh told them that none of them were sticking their fingers in her vagina and to not even consider it. Then she scolded Sorcha for being so crass in front of

MJ. They all looked at the little girl, who still had an iron grip on Charlie's hand.

"It's okay. Sorcha is a little like Luna. My dad said Luna had no filter. I don't think Sorcha has a filter either."

They all laughed then, though there was no easing any of the tension in the room. Gavin had gone back to pacing, not even glancing up at the laughter, and Nessa wondered if he was jonesing for a fix. If that was the case, then soon enough, Gavin would become even more volatile. And when Gavin lost his temper, Nessa tended to bear the brunt of his anger.

She was okay with that once everyone else stayed safe.

Nessa closed her eyes and found herself remembering one of the times Gavin had taken his anger out on her.

Nessa knew she was late. That Gavin would already be home, and she should have been home long before him. He got mad when she wasn't waiting for him when he got home. Nessa hadn't meant to stay out till now, but she had sat in the pub for the entire afternoon, listening to music, and chatting to people her own age.

It was the middle of fresher's week, when all the new college students descended on pubs and clubs in town and had the time of their lives. Nessa had always wondered what her first year in college would be like, would she make new friends or would she cling to her childhood friends?

But Gavin hadn't wanted her to go to college.

God, she wished she had tried to talk him round, to let her go and have that experience but when Gavin told her something, Nessa had to agree or face the wrath of his anger. She paused with her hand on the door of their apartment, glancing at the empty hallway and wondering if she could just turn around and walk away.

She had nowhere else to go.

Gavin was all she had.

Steeling herself, Nessa opened the door and strode inside, kicking off her shoes, and setting her handbag down. There wasn't a sound inside the apartment and for one, blissful moment, Nessa relaxed thinking she'd beat Gavin home.

"Where were you?"

Nessa whirled around to see Gavin sitting on the edge of the couch, half a bottle of wine in his hand. She walked into the living room and gave Gavin the excuse that she had rehearsed over and over on the way home.

"I was in town, and I missed my bus. I had to wait for the next one and it took ages. Traffic was mental. I'm sorry I'm late."

Gavin lifted his gaze to hers. "Do you think I'm an idiot?"

"It's the truth." Nessa lied, her heart galloping in her chest.

Gavin lunged off the couch, dropping the bottle of wine. He grabbed her by the throat, and shoved her hard against the wall. "Don't. fucking. Lie. To. Me."

His fingers dug into her throat and Nessa wondered if he was strong enough to crush her throat. His pupils were blown so she knew he was stoned, and she tried to stay very, very still in his grasp.

"Denzo saw you hanging out with all the college freaks. Said you were really cosy with some blonde dude who looked like he wanted to fuck you. He said you were smiling at him like you didn't belong to someone else."

"No. I went in to have a drink while waiting for my bus. The fella in the bar was just being nice. I told him I was with someone. If Denzo had kept watching, he would have seen me run for the bus. That's the truth."

Gavin didn't look like he was buying her lies, and panic flooded her chest, pain striking her and she felt like she was gonna pass out. He watched her, looking for anything that would betray her. Then he leaned in and bit down hard on her jaw.

Nessa cried out, her skin stinging. That only seemed to encourage Gavin more. He ripped the front of her shirt, then bit down hard on her shoulder. Nessa sucked in a breath, as Gavin's bite was rough enough to break her skin. She could smell the copper in the air.

She had to endure this biting, this marking, this humiliation for thirty minutes as Gavin left his teeth marks on her skin. He had stripped her naked while doing so, then stepped back and admired his work.

"You look so damn sexy wearing my mark."

Nessa locked down her emotions. She knew what was coming next. Knew it the moment she had felt his growing erection pressed against her stomach as he had bitten her. Nessa closed her eyes and blocked it all out.

Or at least she tried to.

Nessa snapped her eyes open to see Gavin watching her.

She adverted her gaze as Niamh grabbed her stomach. "Something doesn't feel right."

Cliona helped Sorcha over to where Niamh was, the blonde woman holding Niamh's gaze as she told her. "Yano, I've done this a few times. I mean, it was normally helping my dad calf heifers or foal a filly, but it's got to be the same right?"

"Are you calling me a fucking heifer, Sorcha?" Niamh accused her friend through gritted teeth.

"Um nope, didn't mean to. But let me have a look and then we can see if my farmgirl knowledge stacks up."

Sorcha waited until Niamh gave her a shaking nod of her head, then Sorcha lifted the blanket and dipped her head. The other woman frowned, then lifted her head.

"Okay, so there is a little blood. I need to get real intimate with you and check and see if I can feel the baby's head. It's probably not going to be comfortable and won't feel as nice as having Oli down there but I'm all you got."

"Are you deliberately saying shit to distract me?"

Sorcha grinned. "Yup. Is it working?"

Niamh rolled her eyes, letting her head thunk back against the counter. "Just do it. Please, Sorcha."

Sorcha's face got very serious, and she dipped her head down. Nessa watched Niamh flinch, her hand clenching Charlie's. Sorcha spent a long time being quiet, which wasn't like the woman. Then Nessa saw her lift her head and there was a look of pure terror in Sorcha's eyes for a moment before it vanished, and Niamh looked back at her.

"Sorcha?"

Sorcha took a deep breath. "Right, so we are gonna need you to not push, honey. Not even a little. Mini Scott has decided they want to make their entrance into the world feet first and that's not good. I know it's gonna feel awful but I'm gonna keep my hand where it is for now."

Niamh started to cry, a cascade of tears flowing from her eyes. "My baby's gonna die. Oh god, don't let them die."

It was the closest to keening Nessa had ever heard as Niamh sobbed and Cliona and Charlie hugged her carefully. Sorcha looked bereft from her position between Niamh's legs. She looked at Nessa, and in that moment, Nessa knew that if Niamh didn't get to the hospital soon, they might lose them both.

White-hot anger flooded her veins, and made her shoot out of her seat. That was not going to happen. Nessa had spent too long afraid of Gavin, jumping at shadows, and hiding because of him. No more. She was done being afraid. She was done letting him win.

"Are you really gonna sit there and be the reason why that baby dies? Are you that much of a fucking asshole that you think that you'll walk away this time round? The last time you had daddy to call in favours. This time, these people matter. It's public. You just sit there and let this happen and it proves just how much of a coward you truly fucking are, Gavin."

Gavin slowly got to his feet and raised his arm until the gun was pointed right at her, his hand trembling. "I'll kill you, then, since you don't matter."

Nessa felt herself smile. "That's the problem, Gavin. I do matter. I matter to these women. I matter to them. I matter to a man who is a hundred times more of a man than you are. You kill me and I'll still matter. But you. It's you that doesn't matter, and I don't think you ever did."

Chapter Twenty-Five

Darren

James started to strip off his jacket, then his jumper, and his belt. Darren quirked his brow, amused at the other man. "What's with the Magic Mike routine?"

"I walk in there dressed like a guard," James said with a flicker of amusement in his eyes, "and the motherfucker is likely to shoot me. No matter who else he might want to shoot, laying eyes on the badge is nearly a surefire way to end up with a bullet. Besides, I get shot and me ma will kill me. Or my brothers. So better safe than sorry."

Huh, ya that made sense.

James shoved his discarded clothing to the side, then rose to input the code for the door. The light on the panel flashed green, then he turned the handle, and the door opened without making a sound. James held a finger to his lips, and Darren might have rolled his eyes if adrenaline didn't feel like a fire in his veins.

They crept inside the basement of the shop, crossing the floor quickly. They could hear raised voices upstairs, and Darren felt a sense of dread as he heard Gavin say. "I'll kill you, then, since you don't matter."

He could almost see the smile on Nessa's face as she replied. "That's the problem, Gavin. I do matter. I matter to these women. I matter to them. I matter to a man who is a hundred times more of a man than you are. You kill me and I'll still matter. But you. It's you that doesn't matter, and I don't think you ever did."

Yes, Nessa fucking mattered to him. Thank fuck she knew that.

His gaze locked with James', the other man motioning with his head that he was heading up the stairs. Darren nodded, then took up behind James so that he could follow him. The layout of the bookstore meant that the stairs to the basement was off to the side of the shop, so that when they reached the top of the stairs, they would be shielded from Gavin's view by the bookshelves.

They kept to the walls as they reached the top, and James pointed to the second-level balcony, the study area where he and Nessa had started to fall for one another. James beckoned him closer, then whispered. "I'm gonna go up and try and take him from behind.

You think you can draw his attention to you so we might blindside him."

Darren grinned. "I'm a fucking expert at causing a distraction."

"Just don't get shot," James said to him, still talking in a low murmur.

"You either. I don't want your ma to kill me for getting her son shot."

James smiled, then swiftly climbed up and over the railing, and then gave Darren a thumbs up. Knowing this was probably a terrible idea, Darren braced himself and took a step out into the open.

"Is this a private party or can anyone join in?"

Nessa whirled round to stare at him, her eyes wide. MJ cried out his name, and he smiled at her before turning back to the man with the gun. His body was angled in a way that he'd see James out of the corner of his eye if Darren didn't get him moved, so Darren took another few steps forward.

"You must be Gavin."

"And you must be the prick fucking my woman."

Darren glanced at Nessa, and flashed her a grin. "Nessa's her own woman. She doesn't belong to me, and she certainly doesn't belong to you. bet that gets your nuts all in a twist, right Gav?"

Just like Darren intended, Gavin shifted his arm, so the gun was pointed at Darren. It also inched him closer to the angle Darren needed his body to be at so that James could do his thing.

"I broke her. she's mine."

Darren let loose a mocking chortle. "Dude, if you think you broke her, then you are as dumb as you look."

Nessa sucked in a breath and Gavin looked at her, then back at Darren. "Maybe I'll kill you then, make her watch as you bleed out. That will break her. That will finish her off, knowing that she's the reason why you're dead."

Darren gave a little shrug of his shoulders. "You pull the trigger, Gav, and you're the reason why I'm dead. Not Nessa. But if I die, she'll know that I love her. That I came in here so she would know that she is loved. Every single piece of her is loved."

Nessa was crying now, but Darren had to ignore that as he walked a little closer and Gavin's hand shook. Maybe it was the adrenaline, maybe it was because he was a fecking idiot, but he wasn't afraid when he knew that he should be.

Darren glanced over at Niamh, at the women trying to keep the woman as calm as they could. He looked back at Gavin, tilting his head. "Does it get ya off, Gav, hurting women? Does it make you feel like more of a man to have them at your mercy? I mean, personally, I think it's a little bitch move. You are such a stereotype. You hate strong women. But let me tell ya, Gav, I was raised by a strong woman. I can see that strength in all of these women."

A muscle in Gavin's jaw ticked, and his lips twisted

into a scowl. Ya, Darren was getting on his nerves. Good. He wanted to needle him and provoke him so that he would focus solely on Darren and forget about everyone else in the room.

"I'm also the man I am because of the men in my life. First, it was a bear of a man who took me under his wing, and gave me brothers and a sister. Gave me a niece who I adore. You can't even fucking compare to any of them. Nessa was right when she called you a coward. The inmates are gonna have a great time breaking you in prison."

Darren moved so that he was standing in front of Nessa, her hand gripping the back of his t-shirt as she said softly. "I love you too, Darren."

Gavin moved so that his back was to the steps, the gun pointed at Darren. "I will shoot you."

"Then just do it. You are all talk and no action, Gav. I bet you suffer from small dick syndrome, right? Let me guess, you drive a Merc?"

Gavin's face went bright red, the gun shaking in his trembling hand. Darren laughed, hoping to cover James as he glanced from around a bookcase. "Ah mate, shit. I knew it. I mean, I'm pretty good at reading people. Comes with the job. I can tell ya now that you can't handle a little bit of pain. You'd pass out before the needle was on your skin, probably at the sound of the machine starting up."

"You don't know anything about me!" Gavin roared, and Nessa grabbed his t-shirt tighter.

Darren let go of the easy-going façade and folded his arms across his chest. "I do know ya Gav. I know that you preyed on a teenage girl and forced her to keep your secrets. You were the adult in this. Then you used your fists to control her."

Darren wanted to hurt the man in front of him so badly. But as much as he wanted to show Gavin exactly how much pain he couldn't take, Nessa didn't need him to be like Gavin. She needed him to be Darren.

"You used the fact that she was desperate to be loved. Yano, if she had been raised by parents who loved her, she wouldn't have looked at you twice. Sure, you might be reasonably good looking, and have money, but Nessa would never have been happy to stay in your world. She shines so bright, it's like the sun on your skin. Who the fuck could you have wanted to take that feeling away?"

James had stepped out from the bookcase, and inclined his head as he came down the steps. Darren lowered his voice, and whispered to Nessa. "When I move, drop to the floor."

She let go of his tee, and then James got to the bottom step. As if he sensed someone behind him, Gavin began to turn. Darren shouted for Nessa to get down, then he dove for Gavin, grabbing him by the waist as James wrapped his arms around Gavin's chest. Gavin jerked his head back, catching James in the chin, and Gavin tried to swing his arm around.

They tackled Gavin at the same time, bringing him

down to the ground. Darren could hear all the women behind them, and knew they needed to disarm Gavin as quickly as possible. Gavin raked his nails down Darren's face, and Darren hissed out a curse.

James had his knee on Gavin's chest, his hand straining to reach for Gavin's hand.

And that was when the gun went off.

Chapter Twenty-Six

Nessa

HAVING DROPPED to the ground the moment Darren told her to, Nessa pushed up onto her knees, her gaze darting round to try and figure out if anyone was shot. Her heart was in her throat as she watched James punch Gavin in the face, and then slam his hand into the floor.

The gun fell from Gavin's hand, and then Cliona was there, kicking it away as the two men wrestled Gavin. They managed to get him on his stomach, and James had Gavin's hands behind his back as Darren lay over his legs to hold him in place.

Cliona rushed over to the door as Nessa got to her feet, the other woman unlatching the door as she flung it open. "We need help!"

Nessa's legs threaten to buckle as she tries to step

out of the way of the police and paramedics who come rushing in. One of the paramedics looked achingly similar to James, and she knew it must be one of his brothers.

"James, you get shot?"

"Nah, I'm grand. Shot went into the wall."

"Good, 'cause mam would kill us both if you got shot."

There was a flurry of movement as Sorcha explained that the baby was feet first, and she was doing all that she could to stop the feet from coming out. James's brother got down on the ground, gave Sorcha's shoulder a squeeze. "Get yourself looked at, blondie. You did good."

Then he turned his attention to Niamh. "Hey, Niamh. I'm Connor. That idiot over there is my brother and we are also Declan's younger and more handsome brothers. I'm gonna have a look at you, if that's okay, and see if I can nudge your kiddo in the right direction."

Nessa turned away as other guards hauled Gavin up, his eyes clashing with hers.

"I'll kill you. I'll find you and kill you!"

Then Gavin was gone, dragged out as the paramedics loaded Niamh onto a trolley, and then they were moving, Connor shouting for people to move outta the fucking way.

Charlie had MJ still in her embrace as they stayed where they were, more ambulance crew coming in to take Sorcha to hospital. Cliona went with her, as Darren held out his fist to James, who bumped it, then told Darren to go get his girl.

Darren hugged Nessa to him, as the shock started to take hold and she was shaking, but she lifted her head to see James crouch down in front of MJ. "Hey MJ, do you remember me?"

"You're Declan's brother. You came to help when Hannah overdosed."

James wiped the blood from his nose. "That's me. How bout you give me a hug and we can go and make sure your dad's okay. He's been a little worried."

MJ looked at Charlie, who nodded to MJ, and MJ immediately wrapped her arms around James's neck, and then buried her face in his neck. James got to his feet and carried MJ with ease. There was no way that if anyone snapped a picture of the guard striding out the door, his face bloody, carrying the little girl in his arms that it wouldn't be front page news.

Nessa told someone to make sure Molly was okay as she was still in the office.

It was then that Nessa realized that Charlie hadn't gotten up yet. The other women started to cry, and Nessa slipped from Darren's arms, to go to her. "Charlie?"

"I'm okay, I'm okay. I have cramps."

Oh no...

Without another word, Darren came over and

scooped Charlie up in his arms. "I got ya. There is no way that prick gets to take a fucking life today."

Charlie looked stunned as Darren walked her out in his arms, telling her Cliona had put her phone in MJ's pocket so they could hear everything. Charlie's expression changed to panic, but Darren said. "No one is gonna tell, Noah. We just need to make sure you're okay."

Darren stepped out into the street, and Nessa heard Andi Collins call her best friend's name. the severity of what had happened must have hit Charlie suddenly because her eyes rolled back in her head, and she fainted.

When someone wheeled a stretcher over, Darren told them calmly that Charlie had fainted and that she was pregnant, though they weren't sure how far along she was. Andi came forward, relief on her face as Nessa explained what had happened.

Then the ambulances were all pulling away and Nessa stood in the street, surveying the chaos that Gavin had caused. That *she* had caused.

Hands cupped her face. "Hey, it's all gonna be okay."

Nessa wasn't sure that she believed him. They would all hate her, wouldn't they, if something happened it Niamh and the baby. To Charlie. What had almost happened to MJ?

Shifting her head, Nessa looked at MJ cradled against her dad as Ciara hugged James. Isaac was crying, his hand on MJ's head. When a photographer tried to take a picture, Cathal stepped forward and put his hand over the camera. James ordered the cameras away, then said something to Isaac who nodded.

James came over to them. "I'm driving Isaac and MJ to the hospital, just so she can get a once over. Cathal said he'd take you and Nessa."

"I'm fine," Nessa argued because in the grand scheme of things, her trauma was nothing compared to what everyone else was going through.

"Even so," Darren said as he kissed her forehead. "We can get you checked out; I'll have someone look at the chicken scraws on my face, and then we can check on everyone else."

Nessa let Darren walk her over to where Cathal had his car parked, as Darren opened the passenger seat and let her sit in. She felt numb. She felt like she was running on empty. Darren got in behind her, and then Cathal was driving off toward the hospital.

Nessa stared out the window, scanning the people who walked by like they hadn't a care in the world. It was hard to believe that while the last few hours had seemed to stop time for her, the rest of the world carried on around them.

She wondered if Niamh would want her to move out now and would fire her. She had been the reason why Gavin was at the store, why he'd done what he'd done. Why the happy place where Nessa felt most at home would now feel tainted by Gavin's touch, much like she felt now.

Would it ever be over?

"You scared the shit out of me when you ran off to play hero," Cathal said suddenly breaking the silence, and Nessa shifted so that she looked at the other man.

"I wasn't trying to play hero, Hoggy."

Cathal ran a hand down his face, lifting his gaze to the mirror so Darren could see his eyes. "I know. Still scared me though. But you know what?"

"What?" Darren's tone was clipped like he was expecting a lecture from his surrogate big brother.

"I've never been prouder of you." Cathal's voice cracked as he spoke, and Nessa reached over and put her hand on his arm.

"But I swear if you give me any more grey hairs like that, I'll sic Luna on ya."

Darren chuckled, and Nessa could hear the emotion in his tone even as he joked. "I dunno, Hoggy. I think Luna might like you as a silver fox."

"Don't you dare tell her that."

They arrived at the hospital, where James met them at the door and insisted that Nessa get checked out. He asked Darren to give him a few minutes with Nessa, and Darren kissed her quickly on the lips, telling her he'd be outside when she was done.

"We gotta stop meeting like this." James joked when they were alone.

"You've gotta stop saving me," Nessa replied,

knowing that was twice now that James had come to save her.

"Nah, that was all Darren. I just followed his lead. Wanted to keep him safe for you."

Nessa offered him a sad smile. "I love him. if any of it matters after what I've caused."

James reached out and touched her cheek. "Like I told you last time, this is not on you. it's Gavin's fault. Everyone knows that."

Nessa let loose a sob, and James held her to him for a time. Then she felt James untangle himself from her and then Darren was holding her, and she instantly felt safe. Nessa buried her face in his chest, letting out all her guilt, her sadness, her pain in the tears as if she could finally grieve for the girl she had been once, and finally put her to bed.

That was the thing about survival; you didn't believe you'd actually done it even when you had. You expected the worst at all times. You hoped for the best but prepared for the worst. Back then, Nessa had been alone. She had no one to help her survive. Now she had a real man who loved her, friends who had become her family, and maybe, just maybe, Nessa could take the chance and live her life again.

CHAPTER TWENTY-SEVEN

Nessa

WHEN THE HOSPITAL realized that their public waiting area was full to the brim with famous people, and it was drawing a pretty large crowd, they moved them all to a private waiting area up near the maternity section. They were all eager to hear any news on Niamh and the baby, and as time ticked by, Nessa had a knot in her stomach.

Issac was the first to come in with MJ and Ciara, refusing to be parted from his daughter even when Cathal offered to take her, like he was afraid of letting her out of his sight again. Cathal then offered to take them home, but Isaac shook his head.

"MJ refused to go home until she knew all her friends were okay."

The door opened and Cliona wheeled Sorcha in,

her friend grinning as Nessa looked horrified at the boot that went to her knee from her foot. Danika jumped up and kissed Cliona hard, and Sorcha sighed, wheeling herself forward.

"They see me rolling, they hatin'."

Darren barked out a laugh, shaking his head. "She's way worse than I am."

"Sorcha has no filter like Luna," MJ said, lifting her head from her dad's shoulder.

Cathal scrubbed a hand down his face, then looked at Sorcha. "I'm gonna try and keep you two apart for my own sanity."

That made Sorcha laugh, and then she winced. "Oh fuck, bruised ribs are not fun. Do not recommend."

Nessa's chest ached. She wanted to apologise, she wanted to tell Sorcha that she was so sorry for all the pain she was in. Her lips parted, the words stuck in her throat as the door at the far end of the hall opened and Charlie and Andi came out. Everyone turned to look at them, taking in Charlie's pale face and Nessa's heart almost sank to the floor.

Please, if there is any higher power, let her be okay.

"I'm okay. We're okay. Please don't say anything to Noah."

As if she had conjured him, Noah burst through the door and almost collided with Cliona and Danika. His eyes latched on to Charlie and then they were rushing toward each other. Noah embraced Charlie, and Nessa looked away when she heard Noah say in the husky tone of his.

"I thought I'd lost you. I can't lose you, Charlie."

"I'm okay. I promise I'm okay."

A throat cleared behind the couple and they broke apart to see Isaac standing there, having finally handed MJ off to Cathal. He stood there looking at Charlie for a minute, then shook his head before he began to speak. "I watched you on that video feed. You put yourself in between my daughter and that madman. You shielded her as if she was your own. She told me that she wasn't too scared because you held her hand. I can never repay that debt, Charlie. Just thank you."

Charlie stepped forward and gave Issac a hug, and she said something very low that Nessa couldn't hear. When they separated, they were both crying. Noah pulled Charlie to him again, and then they all took a seat and waited for more news.

Connor, the paramedic stopped by to check on everyone, flirted with Sorcha a little, and that had them all laughing. They drank terrible coffee until Andi threw on her get shit done hat and ordered coffee and food to be delivered. Nessa nibbled on her sandwich, not in the least bit hungry.

Cliona had fallen asleep in Danika's lap. MJ was asleep in Cathal's. Charlie and Noah had taken to the seats a couple of rows back, and were taking quietly.

Every so often, someone passed through the corridor, saw the famous rockstar, the F1 driver, and stuttered to a stop. Darren and Isaac started taking bets on how many nurses fancied Danika, and how many had goo goo eyes for Noah. Then Ciara chimed in and said she wanted in with how many nurses fancied them both.

Cathal told them all to grow up, which made everyone laugh, and it seemed to take with it, the intensity that had everyone on tenterhooks. Andi was walking the halls, answering her phone, making plans, and offering brief one-line statements.

Then her phone rang, and a small smile curved her lips. "Hey handsome."

Declan must have said something down the phone, 'cause Andi laughed, then sobered. "No. We are still waiting. I'll give ya a shout when I have news. How's Jameson holding up?"

Jameson and Niamh were as close as any siblings could be, and he worried a lot about Niamh. It must be killing him to be too far aware to be here for his sister.

"Okay...Charlie is sending the plane over to Manchester to get you guys. I have one of our guys, Shane acting as point to make sure you guys get back ASAP. Tell Shane I said that if he wants to come home and talk about that job offer, then there's a seat on the plane for him. Hell, get Luna to drag his ass on the plane so he can stop avoiding my calls."

Then Andi laughed. "Ya, ya. I love you too. See ya later."

Andi had just hung up the phone when the door directly opposite the seating area opened. Oli strode out, shirtless, and barefoot, which was probably against all health regulations. He had the biggest grin on his face, cradling a little bundle to his chest. One hand was on the end of the blanket, the other on the baby's head.

Everyone came to attention.

"Everyone is doing okay. Niamh told me to come out and tell ya all that she is doing grand and that mini-Scott was worth every ounce of pain. She was a fucking warrior, was my fiancée."

"Oh praise Jesus you finally asked her!" Danika exclaimed.

Oli grinned, and Nessa felt herself smiling along with him. "I was waiting for the perfect moment, but the second I knew my two girls were okay, it felt like the right time."

Tears filled Danika's eyes. "A girl? I have a niece?"

"Yup. I'm gonna be surrounded by strong females and I am here for it." Oli shifted the baby in his arms and finally showed her off. "Ladies and heathens, let me introduce you formally to Indigo, Jaymes Scott."

Danika narrowed her gaze. "Jaymes?"

Oli rolled his eyes, but he was laughing. "Well, you and Jameson got to be godparents. And before you have a go at me, my future wife picked Jaymes. I suggested Indigo."

MJ got up off her seat and came over to where Oli

was standing. The rockstar crossed his legs and lowered himself down to the ground, so that MJ could get a closer look. Nessa almost melted when she heard Oli say. "My two favourite girls."

MJ beamed as Oli pulled down the blanket so MJ could see Indigo a little better.

"Hi Indie, I'm MJ." Issac's daughter said, and Nessa could see the resilience in the little girl, because she was loved, she was protected, and her future was limitless.

"I'm going to look after you like Uncle Cathal looks after my dad, and Darren and Shay. You can be my little sister if you like. And even when I get my own brother or sister, I'll still love you. Because that's what family does."

"Fuck, I'm leaking again," Oli said, leaning forward to kiss MJ's forehead.

Issac got up and came over, lifting his daughter into his arms.

"Daddy, you're squishing me too tight again."

"I know, MJ, I'm not sorry though."

Oli got back to his feet saying he'd better call Jameson. He looked at all the people in the waiting area. "Go home and get some rest folks. I'll send regular updates on my girls. Today, let's just soak in the good of the day and leave any ugliness behind. And before anyone starts to blame themselves for what happened, the only person to blame is the man who came in wielding a gun."

His gaze shifted to Nessa, and she shifted under the scrutiny. "Niamh said you'd blame yourself. She doesn't. I don't. And in time, when we tell Indigo about the day she came into this world and how her auntie Nessa stood in front of a loaded gun to protect her mam, neither will she."

Nessa didn't know what to say to that and she stared after Oli dumbstruck. She didn't even speak as Darren led her to Cathal's car. Darren placed his hands on either side of her face, and brushed his lips against her forehead. "I'll take you home."

Shaking her head, Nessa replied to Darren. "I can't go back there yet. Tomorrow. Take me anywhere else but there."

Darren kissed her quickly on the lips, brushing her hair from her eyes. "No hassle. I'm gonna take ya home to mine. Or we could crash at Cathal's if you'd prefer."

No, Rebel Ink was still too close. For tonight, she wanted to be anywhere else.

The place didn't really matter, once she was in Darren's arms.

Chapter Twenty-Eight

Darren

Darren stared at the ceiling, afraid to move in case he woke Nessa. He'd taken her to his home early in the morning, and had offered to take the couch, but she had just asked him to hold her, because then she would know she was safe.

And so that's what he'd done, just held her, through her tears, through her nightmare, and when she'd eventually settled, Darren had still held her. As he lay awake, careful not to wake her, Darren wondered what his Gran would think of Nessa. She would be horrified at the abuse that Nessa had suffered. Then she would have gotten mad as all hell and done all she could to make sure Nessa was looked after.

She loved her strays, did his Gran.

He wasn't sure what the future held for him and

Nessa, but Darren was absolutely certain that he wanted to be with her. However, he also didn't want to scare her by being too intense. He needed her to know that he was nothing like Gavin. He wouldn't force Nessa to be with him if that's not what she wanted.

Nessa had told him she loved him when Gavin had a gun pointed at him.

It might have been something Nessa had said in the heat of the moment.

Nessa stirred in his arms, rolled over to blink her eyes awake and then she was looking at him with those intense green eyes watching him. "Morning."

"Morning."

With her lips curving into a smile, Nessa leaned up as if to kiss him, then froze. She had a panicked look in her eyes as she sat upright in the bed, and glanced away.

"Hey, what just happened?" Darren asked her, reaching over to take her hand.

Nessa worried at her bottom lip. "It's stupid, really."

"Well, I've been known to do and say a lot of stupid things so it would be nice to share the honour with ya."

Nessa gave him a coy smile. "Gavin hated kissing in the morning unless I'd brushed my teeth. I would have to wake up an hour before he was due to get up, brush my teeth, fix my hair. But no make-up. He didn't want me to tart myself up."

Darren really wished he had knocked Gavin around a bit before the guards took him away.

"Well, first of all, Gavin's an idiot. I for one think you look gorgeous with your hair sticking at all weird angles, and your eyes all sleepy. Even with that morning breath, I would never turn down a kiss from you."

He leaned down and kissed her quickly on the mouth, then rolled out of bed. Darren stretched, then turned back around to see a genuine smile on Nessa's face.

Ya, he'd never get fucking tired of seeing that.

"I'm gonna stick the kettle on and then maybe we can head out for breakfast? Or brunch at this stage?"

Nessa blinked, and tucked a strand of hair behind her ear. "It's weird to think that I can just go outside now. Like I can go out by myself and not be afraid that Gavin is lurking down some dark alley. I think that will take some getting used to."

"Well, any time you need an emotional support Darren, then I'm your man."

He left her to her thoughts then, heading downstairs and pulling on the tee he'd grabbed on his way out. Darren filled the kettle and turned it on, then checked his phone for any messages. He had one from James, telling him that Gavin had appeared in court this morning and the judge had denied him bail. He'd be in prison pending his trial.

That was good news.

Darren hoisted himself up on the breakfast bar as

he heard light footsteps on the stairs. He filled the mugs when the kettle boiled, and then smiled when Nessa came in wearing one of his t-shirts over her leggings.

"Hey, I had a text from James. Gavin was refused bail. He's gonna be locked up until his trial."

Nessa was quiet for a few minutes. She walked into the kitchen, and leaned on the counter opposite him. "I should feel relieved. I should be doing one hell of a happy dance. But I just feel numb to it all. Like this is a dream and when I wake up, I'll be back there, in that apartment with him trying to kill me."

Darren held out his hand. Nessa slipped her fingers into his.

"Gavin is finally getting what he deserves. The world is yours again."

Nessa looked confused as she seemed to ponder his words. "I wouldn't know where to start. My life has been consumed with staying hidden. Of drifting under the radar and not making plans. I honestly thought that at some point Gavin would eventually succeed in killing me so there was no use in making plans."

Darren gave her hand a little pull, not hard enough that she wouldn't be able to stay where she was if she didn't want to come to him. Nessa came forward, put her hands on his thighs, and he ran his hands up and down her arms.

"It's never too late to be who you want to be. Gavin doesn't get to control you any more. So, Nessa

Kennedy, now that you get to take on the world, what do you want to do?"

Darren kept rubbing her arms, letting her come to terms with the fact that her life was hers now. She tapped her fingers on his thighs, and Darren gave her the space to think things over.

"College," Nessa said, lifting her gaze to his. "I always wanted to go to college. I'm a different person than I was before, so my old interests don't fit me. I think I'd like to help others like me, in times, when I've had time to process everything."

"Jameson's Sinéad is the one you need to talk to. She's qualified in all that stuff.

Nessa smiled at him. "I had forgotten. I'll speak to her."

"She might also put you in touch with people who have been in similar situations."

Anxiety flashed in her eyes and then it was gone.

"I want to move on with my life. I don't know if Niamh and Sorcha will want me working for them after all this, but Rebel Books became my safe haven. I want to stay working there. But I will offer them my resignation because I don't want them to feel guilty for letting me go. I understand why they would need to."

Sliding his arms up her arms to rest on Nessa's shoulders, Darren tried to reassure her. "You heard Oli at the hospital. No one is blaming ya, Nessa."

"Oli was all high from the baby fumes."

"Even so," Darren replied with a chuckle. "It's still the truth."

Nessa didn't look like she really believed him, but he would work on building her confidence up little by little, until she saw just how amazing she really was. Even after all of the trauma and abuse, Nessa was still standing. She was strong. She was resilient. And she was beautiful inside and out.

"There's something else I've decided too."

Darren tilted his head, and gave her a lopsided smile. "Oh ya, go on, tell me."

A faint tinge of pink tinged her cheeks. "I'm tired of being alone. I want to give us a shot. All I ever wanted was someone in my life who made me feel wanted, who made me feel special. I was looking for that when I met Gavin. I thought all men were like Gavin."

Darren studied her as she took a deep breath, then lifted her hand to lightly cup his cheek. "But then I met you and you were kind. You made me smile and you validated how I was feeling. You never made me feel like I was damaged goods, Darren."

His heart was racing, because without knowing it, Nessa was doing the same for him. Darren had always known that his Gran loved him, that his Rebel Ink family loved him. Hell, even his cousin Eve loved him. But his parents' attitude to him had bruised his heart more than he cared to let on, and he'd covered it with humour and a cheeky smile.

Nessa made him feel like he was wanted.

"I need to find my feet by myself," Nessa continued dragging Darren from his thoughts. "I need to learn how to not be afraid. How to walk out in the sunshine and not jump at shadows. But I want to know that I can call you if I am overwhelmed. That I can ask you for help and you will be there, like some tattooed knight."

Darren snorted, a little embarrassed. "You make me sound like some swoon-worthy hero from a book. I'm not a hero, Nessa. I'm just a normal guy."

Nessa smiled, warm and welcoming. "I meant every word I said, Darren. I want us. I want you. And I would very much like it now if you would take me to bed so that I can show you just how much I want you."

Chapter Twenty-Nine

Nessa

IT WOULD TAKE some getting used to...this freedom to be out during the day.

A week had passed since the events at Rebel Books. The shop had remained closed and Cliona had called her to say that they were keeping the shop shut for a few weeks. Nessa had offered to go in and clean up, but Cliona had told her that Oli had hired some fancy crew to come and sort the place out.

Nessa had gone back to her apartment a couple of days ago, and Darren had stayed with her, leaving only when he had to go to work. She had started to lean on him, a little too much until one day she had a massive panic attack when they made to leave to go over to have dinner.

She couldn't go out the door. Her chest had

constricted and she could not get air in her lungs. Her knees had trembled before they buckled and Darren had been there to catch her. He had held her, talking to her until she could breathe again. Nessa had never been so ashamed in all her life but Darren had told her that it was a blip, that if she hadn't of had a reaction to everything that went on, then she wouldn't be human.

They'd ordered takeout, and when night fell, Darren had asked her if she wanted to try again. It had been easier that time, in the dark. The darkness had been her friend for so long that it made her feel at ease in it.

Darren had been right, of course. It was hard for her to see how she could ever be normal again. If she was too twisted up inside to find the light, find goodness in the world again. But Darren was good. He was a sliver of light in the dark that threatened to consume her.

A few days later, as they lay in bed, Nessa had gotten a text from Niamh asking her to call round to see her. She told her that Cliona and Sorcha would be there too. Nessa was worried that Niamh was about to fire her.

Darren had offered to go with her, but Nessa was determined to face it by herself. Gavin had never let her get a driver's licence, or learn how to drive, which Nessa wanted to rectify. She let Darren go off to work, and called herself a taxi. They travelled to where Oli and Niamh lived. Nessa was not surprised to see a few photographers lingering outside the big gates.

Getting out of the taxi after paying, Nessa kept her head down as she pressed the button on the intercom. She almost jumped out of her skin when a man appeared out of nowhere.

"I'm sorry to scare ya." He said with a smile. "Names, Gus. I'm Oli's head of security. Come on in, Nessa."

Gus pulled open the gates and Nessa slipped in, heading for the door when Gus told her it was unlocked. She paused with her hand on the door knob, taking a deep breath before she rapped her knuckles on the door, and called out a quiet hello.

Oli came striding from the kitchen, the biggest smile on his face. "Hey Nessa, all the girls are in the sitting room. Head away in. Can I get you something to drink?"

"No, thank you. I don't think I'll be staying long."

Oli's gaze narrowed, his lips curving downward into a frown, but he didn't say anything. Instead, he led her into the living room, then reached over and gave her shoulder a squeeze.

Everyone turned in her direction, and a sudden wave of panic made her dizzy.

This had been a bad idea.

She wanted to leave but she was frozen to the spot.

She felt the wetness on her cheeks and knew that she was crying.

Niamh, who had been cradling her daughter in her arms, handed Indigo to Danika, and slowly got to her feet. She came toward Nessa, her face kind, and her eyes, they were full of understanding.

"I won't make you fire me." Nessa blurted out. "I'm giving you my notice."

Niamh's eyes darkened. "Well, you can fuck right off."

Nessa let out a startled laugh, unsure what to do except say. "I almost got you and Indigo killed. I almost got Sorcha killed."

"Not to interrupt or anything," Danika said, as Nessa shifted her gaze to the rockstar. "But Sorcha almost got herself killed by being a smartass."

Sorcha just rolled her eyes and flipped off Danika, who ignored her.

"Danika's right, Nessa." Niamh said to Nessa, and she looked back at the new mother as she continued. "There is only one person to blame and we aren't even gonna mention that asshole's name because he does not deserve any more of our time. Come sit down."

Niamh brushed away Nessa's tears, then took her hand and led her over to where Cliona was sitting beside Sorcha in her wheelchair. Once Nessa had taken a seat, Niamh went back over and took Indigo back from Danika.

"Stop hogging my niece." Danika sighed, jutting out her bottom lip in a mock pout.

"This tiny human came out of my vagina, Dani.

When you push a baby out with no pain meds, then you get to call dibs."

Danika grinned, and glanced at Cliona before she said. "Nah, Cliona's gonna be the birth mom. She's gonna look hot AF all pregnant and shit."

Cliona's mouth hung open, then closed as she went a furious shade of red. *"Danika."*

"Did we not discuss this? I feel like we talked about this. Or was that just in my head?"

Niamh snorted a laugh and the rest of them joined in as Oli came in and handed Nessa a mug of coffee, then went over to Niamh.

"How about me and Indie have some daddy-daughter time and you all can catch up."

Oli scooped his daughter, leaned down to kiss Niamh and then he was striding out, singing softly to Indigo, and Nessa swore she saw Niamh swoon.

"Right, so, if you've stopped making goo goo eyes at your hot rocker, then we should have a chat before Niamh gets her tits out."

Niamh rolled her eyes. "Jesus Christ, Sorcha. Breastfeeding. You already made Jameson blush like a schoolgirl when you said it the other day. Do not say that in front of my dad or I swear, I will hurt you."

"Promises, promises. Right back to business." Sorcha said as she wheeled her chair round a little. "Me and momma bear have been talking and a few things need to change around Rebel Books."

Nessa's heart clenched and she cast her eyes down.

"First of all," Niamh said, leaning forward to take a biscuit, having a nibble before she carried on. "When the shop opens back up, there's a new rotation of shifts coming into effect. Once my maternity leave is up, and Sorcha is back on her feet, we will all take turns working the night shift."

"I don't mind working the night shift." Nessa said softly, but Niamh was already shaking her head.

"No. Everything is gonna be more equal. We can hire more staff. But Nessa, it's only fair. You need to start living your life. And besides, you gotta make time for a certain tattoo artist."

Nessa felt her cheeks heat, and everyone was smiling at her, like they were genuinely happy for her.

"Fitz, he's good people. Goofy at times, but I think you could do with a little goofy, Nessa." Remarked Danika as she came over to sit down beside Cliona and leaned back in the chair.

"What happened last week, he doesn't get to take anything away from us. That means he wins and the little men who try and make us feel less, they don't get to win."

Nessa looked right at Niamh, and saw that her friend meant it. Looking around at the strong women in the room with her, Nessa knew that she had found her family. They had been friends before, but somehow, in the midst of a horrific event, it had cemented their bond.

"So what do we call each other now, this girl gang of ours?" Cliona asked, as Danika chuckled.

"Badass Bitches?" Sorcha offered.

"Bookish Babes?" Niamh said with a massive grin.

"Lame," Cliona rolled her eyes, then she looked at Nessa. "Got any better ideas?"

All Nessa had ever wanted in her life was to feel a part of something. To be loved. To be seen. These women saw her. Darren saw her. They loved her. And Niamh was right. Gavin won if she continued to let him. Nessa knew that every time she did something that she wouldn't have done if Gavin had killed her, when she learned to drive, when she kissed Darren and held his hand in public, Nessa won.

Gavin had stolen enough from her. That stopped now.

Nessa felt the tightness in her chest ease.

"Family. We'll call it family."

CHAPTER THIRTY

Darren

ONE MONTH Later

Well, that was that then.

Darren had gone to a meeting with his Gran's solicitor this morning, and his parents had sent a representative of their interests to the meeting. Darren had dressed in black jeans, and a black shirt that he had buttoned halfway up, though he had rolled up the sleeves. Not that Darren was trying to impress anyone but his gran would have expected him to.

Nessa had offered to go with him, and while Darren had been so tempted to bring her along for support, Nessa was trying very hard to be brave. If she could then so could he.

He sat inside the meeting with his parents on speakerphone and almost laughed his ass off.

Even from the world beyond, his Gran was showing her son and daughter-in-law just how little she thought of them and how they had treated their child. In one fail swoop, thanks to her solicitor if Darren could judge by the smile on his face.

Turns out that his gran had sold the house during the peak of housing to a company that bought houses from people, let them live in the home until their death, then they took possession of the property. His Gran had kept most of the money from the sale in a separate bank account.

In her new revised will that only her solicitor had, his gran had left her son a sum of twenty thousand euros and a watch that belonged to his granddad. His Da had come on the line then and asked what else, only to be told that was all that was in the will for him.

Then came the kick in the nuts to his parents, and when the solicitor read the next part of the will, Darren could almost feel his gran in the room.

"And to my other son, the son that I chose and would always chose, I leave everything else I own. The rest of the money I have is yours, my boy. Don't be sad that you can't stay in our home, but I don't want my ghost to linger. One day, you'll settle down and that money will set you up. Make it a home for family, Darren, even if it's not conventional. Lord knows we were anything but conventional."

Darren had barked out a laugh, earning a glare

from his parent's solicitor, and his Ma to say. "Really, Darren."

Then the solicitor had said. "Final few words from me, Darren. After my Padraig died, I felt this emptiness for the longest time. Then you came into my life and every second that I spent raising you, filled me with joy. You are a good man, a good son, and I loved ya with all my heart. Go live and extraordinary life, my boy."

Darren had been crying by the time the solicitor had finished, but he heard his Da ask if there was a means to contest the amount given to him. His own solicitor piped up that there was nothing they could do or else risk losing everything. His Gran had put a clause in her will that anyone who legally contested the will would end up with nothing.

He had thanked the solicitor and asked him how long he had to get his stuff out of the house. A month. He had a month to pack up all his memories and find somewhere else to live. Even then it would take a few months for the money to be cleared and put into his account.

Darren had stripped off his shirt the moment he was in his car so he looked more like himself when he walked into Rebel Ink. Everyone was at the shop hanging around waiting for him. Shay was sitting on the counter, Isaac was leaning against the wall, and Cathal was sitting in the waiting area.

"Have none of you got any work to do?" Darren said as he flopped down next to Cathal.

"We've all got an amazing boss who knows we wanted to be here for our brother." Cathal had a smirk on his face as Darren rolled his eyes.

"Well, ignoring Cathal," Shay interjected. "What happened?"

Darren scrubbed a hand down his face and told them all what had happened, from his gran's plot twist of a will, to his Da asking if he could contest the amount. He laughed when Shay called them assholes, then just shrugged his shoulders.

"They got more than they deserved, but now it means that I have to move out in a month, find a new gaff to live in, and I won't have any money until for a few months at least."

"You can stay with me, Fitz." Isaac offered, as did Cathal. but Darren didn't wanna play third wheel.

"Nah, I'll just have to take some time to find a place."

"Um, "Shay said looking a little bit embarrassed. "Why don't you move in upstairs?"

Darren shook his head. "Nah, Shay, thanks but I don't wanna third wheel it."

"I've uh, been looking for a time to bring it up but things have been insane and it's not a big deal or anything but Rhys asked me to move in with him, and I was thinking of saying yes as I'm either always there or he's here. So, ya. If Cathal doesn't mind the change in tenant, that is."

Isaac reached over and nudged Shay, who flipped him off.

"Cathal doesn't want to have to deal with me living next to him."

Cathal snorted, rolling his eyes when Darren looked at him. "Yano, probably cause me less stress knowing you're across the hall. Gran would kick my ass for not looking after ya. Besides, Nessa might like having you closer too."

Well, he hadn't really considered that now had he.

Things between him and Nessa were really new, and way too soon for them to be thinking of moving in together. She needed to learn how to be free, and he needed to learn how to be alone without his Gran. But one day, ya, Darren wanted the exact thing that his Gran told him to go in search for...a home...for his family...

But he already had a family.

"I can pay ya rent, Hoggy. I don't want to be a sponger."

Cathal ran his fingers through his hair. "I don't charge family rent. Besides, if Shay is gonna be shacked up with Rhys, then at least I can head away with Luna when she's on tour and know that the shop has someone above it when I'm not here. Oli is getting his guys to hook me up with some proper security, as he put it, that I'm a worrywart and me worrying meant that he didn't have his tattoo artist on tap."

"Is he still thinking about getting some old ink removed so you can give him new ink?"

"Mad bastard that he is he just might."

They all laughed and it looked like the decision had been made. Darren had gone from homeless to a new place in a matter of hours. He was lucky, he was really lucky.

The door to Rebel Ink opened and Nessa walked in. He'd never considered himself a soppy romantic git but when Nessa smiled when he saw him, his heart damn near skipped a beat. Nessa had started to come out of shell slowly, and the last couple weeks, she'd come home after a shopping trip with Cliona with a whole new wardrobe.

Today she wore jeans that hugged her curves and a t-shirt that had a V down the front that showed off her cleavage. She had started to wear a little makeup not that she needed any of that. Nessa could go out in a bin bag and Darren would think she was the most beautiful girl in the world.

Darren sprang up off his seat and strode over to kiss her hard.

It made him grin when he pulled back and Nessa cheeks were a little bit flushed.

"You're in a good mood." Nessa said to him, reaching out to give his arm a squeeze. "It went well?"

"Not well for the parents, and I have to move out in a month, but no worries, Shay is moving in with her rockstar, so Hoggy's gonna let me move in upstairs.

That means I am only across the road when you decide you might want a booty call?"

Cathal, Shay, and Isaac all groaned, but he was deliriously happy.

Nessa laughed, the sound like kisses along his skin., even as her cheeks darkened.

"God, I love you."

Darren froze. Nessa hadn't said it to him since the day at Rebel Books, and he had been content to let her take her time, to find her way to how he felt about her. Nessa, his strong warrior queen who was slaying her demons loved him. There was no hesitation, no caution.

Flashing her a smug, cheeky smile, Darren kissed her, deeper this time to catcalls from his family. He broke the kiss, looked into Nessa's vivid green eyes and said. "I love you too, Nessa."

And he meant every damn word.

THE END

The Rebel County Universe Stories continue in
Take The Lead (Rebel Books Book 3)

Find More Rebel Stories On Kindle Vella

Secrets In Ink is the third novel in the Rebel Ink Trilogy. Rebel Ink is part of the Rebel County Universe which will span at least eight different businesses, with intersecting timelines, and characters popping up when you least expect them.

The Rebel Racers Trilogy
Available Now:
Adrenaline Junkie (Rebel Racers Book 1)
All or Nothing (Rebel Racers Book 2)
Crash and Burn (Rebel Racers Book 3)

The Rebel Rock Trilogy
Available Now:
Centre Stage (Rebel Rock Book 1)
Strings Attached (Rebel Rock Book 2)
Make or Break (Rebel Rock Book 3)

The Rebel Ink Trilogy
Available Now:
Breaking the Habit (Rebel Ink Book 1)
Uncomfortably Numb (Rebel Ink Book 2)
Secrets In Ink (Rebel Ink Book 3)

The Rebel Books Trilogy
Available Now:
Best Laid Plans (Rebel Books Book 1)
More Than Words (Rebel Books Book 2)

Playlists

Darren

Band of Horses - The Funeral

Pierce The Veil - Shared Trauma

Lovejoy - Call Me What You Like

Drake - Started From the Bottom

Stephen Collins - Gimme Your Love

NF - MISTAKE

Labrinth - Never Felt So Alone

James Arthur - A Thousand Years

SLANDER - Wish I Could Forget (with blackbear & Bring Me The Horizon)

VRSTY - D34D

KID BRUNSWICK - Depression

KID BRUNSWICK - Baby I'm Not Okay

Seether - Fake It

Finger Eleven - Paralyzer

All Time Low - Calm Down

The Offspring - Pretty Fly (For A White Guy)

Nothing But Thieves - Keeping You Around

VOILÀ - Don't Say I Didn't Warn You (with Craig Owens)

PVRIS - I DON'T WANNA DO THIS ANYMORE

The Neon Cars - The Way It's Always Been

Eminem - Shake That

All Time Low - Tell Me I'm Alive

Against The Current - "good guy"

Sleeping With Sirens - Complete Collapse

I Prevail - Deep End

About the Author

Susan Harris is a writer from Cork, Ireland and when she's not torturing her readers with heart-wrenching plot twists or killer cliffhangers, she's probably getting some new book related ink, binging her latest TV or music obsession, or with her nose in a book.

Susan LOVES connecting with her fans!
www.susanharrisauthor.com

Nessa

Sarah Proctor - The Breaks

Pierce The Veil - The Jaws Of Life

Jax Jones - Whistle (feat. Calum Scott)

Eminem - Love The Way You Lie

YUNGBLUD - The Funeral

The Neon Cars - Hold Onto It

ILLENIUM - All That Really Matters

grandson - Something To Hide

Matt Hansen - WHERE YOU BELONG

Ruelle - Secrets And Lies

Pierce The Veil - Emergency Contact

Letdown. - Crying In The Shower

Dermot Kennedy - Don't Forget Me

Lily Kershaw - All of the Love in the World

PVRIS - EVERGREEN

VOILÀ - Playing Dead

KID BRUNSWICK - Heaven Without You

Bohnes - Sweet Dream

Taylor Acorn - Coma

Tracy Chapman - Behind the Wall

Hozier - Cherry Wine - Live

Set It Off - Punching Bag

Billie Eilish - What Was I Made For? [From The Motion Picture "Barbie"]

Sleep Token - The Way That You Were

Charlotte Sands - Six Feet Under

Acknowledgments

None of this would be possible without an amazing team supporting me! Many thanks to:

Publishing House: CTP Publishing
Cover design: Gem Promotions
Interior Formating: Gem Promotions

———

And as always:

Thank you to all the readers!
Whether this is your first book by me or you've been with me for years! I only get to do this because of you, and I am eternally grateful to each and every one of you who took a chance on this Irish author.

ALSO BY SUSAN HARRIS

THE WINGS OF DECEIT SERIES

Angel's Gambit, book 1

Angel's Rebel, book 2

Ange's Traitor, book 3

THE EVER CHACE CHRONICLES

Skin & Bones, book 1

Collateral Damage, book 2

Smoke & Mirrors, book 3

Night of the Hunter, book 4

Never Back Down, book 5

Shortcut to the Grave, book 6

Arsonist's Lullaby, book 7

Of Gods & Monsters, book 8

———

SHATTERED MEMORIES

———

Defy The Stars

A Tale of Two Houses, book 1

Until Death Do Us Part, book 2

In Defiance of the Stars, book 3

Courting Darkness, a novella

The Sanguine Crown

Chaos Theory, book 1

Butterfly Effect, book 2

Wicked Game, book 3

Burn Notice, book 4

Fight Song, book 5

The Sicarius Security Series

Kiss Of Death, book 1

Leap Of Faith, book 2

Visions Of Destiny, book 3

War Of Hearts, book 4

Flames Of Conflict, book 5

Anthology

A Lot Like Christmas

www.ingramcontent.com/pod-product-compliance
Lightning Source LLC
Chambersburg PA
CBHW032115170626
46808CB00006B/1951